T0368045

MUTT AND JACK'S EXTRAORDINARY ADVENTURE

JODI DICKEY

authorHOUSE®

AuthorHouse™
1663 Liberty Drive
Bloomington, IN 47403
www.authorhouse.com
Phone: 833-262-8899

Published by AuthorHouse 09/19/2022

ISBN: 978-1-6655-7118-0 (sc)
ISBN: 978-1-6655-7107-4 (e)

Print information available on the last page.

This book is printed on acid-free paper.

This book is dedicated to Mom and Trey.

A BEST FRIEND

Jack Harold Hansen did not like being alone. He had just moved into a new neighborhood in Iceberg, Minnesota, and he did not know any kids who were his age. To make matters worse, school was out for the summer, so he did not have the opportunity to make new friends. Although Jack enjoyed being with his family, he also needed to spend time with his friends to be happy.

Jack wanted friends who were cool and unusual. He needed BFFs to do fun stuff with and go on an adventure.

He thought it was going to be a long, lonely summer without any friends.

Jack was wrong.

One foggy, cool, June morning, Jack was sound asleep, when he was jarred awake from his slumber by the loud ringing of the doorbell. Drowsy, and with his hair all rumpled up,

Jack reluctantly climbed out of his soft, comfortable bed. He walked past the brightly colored hammock that was stretched out across his bedroom and fastened by strong cables to the bedroom walls, donned his cotton, robin's egg blue robe, and walked down the staircase. The doorbell rang again, seemingly more insistent this time, as Jack trudged along the maple hardwood floor in the front entryway of the house.

"I'm coming!" Jack said in a loud, grumpy voice. Jack was not a morning person.

What happened next would change the course of the rest of his life.

Jack opened the front door. Standing outside on the porch was a large, black-and-white, long-haired stray. The dog looked like he needed thorough grooming. The canine pulled back his lips and revealed huge, white teeth.

"Hi, Jack," the dog said as he sat down on the red front porch. Jack's mouth dropped wide open, and his eyes became as large as saucers.

"You can talk!" Jack exclaimed.

"You betcha," the dog answered with his tail wagging and his ears bent forward in excitement and exuberance.

"But how can that be?" Jack asked in a puzzled tone of voice. He stared at the stray for a moment. "I've never met a talking dog before!"

The large canine grinned at the boy with happiness and anticipation.

"I have magical powers," the dog explained, all the while sitting down with his lips pulled back and a huge display of teeth showing. The friendly, exuberant dog paused for a moment. Jack was awestruck by the fact that the dog was sitting there talking to him. "That is how I know your name is Jack." The big dog continued to sit there, his huge, pink tongue lolling out of one side of his mouth.

"Wow!" the 10-year-old finally managed to say, secretly wondering if this was his eyes playing tricks on him. The dog looked at the boy with understanding written all over his face.

"Oh, I assure you this is quite real," explained the large, shaggy, male dog.

"You mean to say you can read my mind, too?" Jack asked with astonishment.

"Yes," the dog simply replied.

"My parents are going to be blown away when they meet you," Jack exclaimed. "A talking dog with magical powers that can also read my mind!" Jack looked at the dog with amazement and newfound respect. An expression of awe appeared on his face.

"That's me!" the dog exclaimed as he wagged his tail. He had a happy expression on his face as he sat there on the porch, grinning at the 10-year-old. "Your job is to convince your parents to let you keep me. Then, I can be your BFF. Also, I will help you to make some new friends who are cool and unusual. After all, that is your heart's desire, right?" the dog asked Jack.

"Yes, that is my most fervent wish!" Jack answered, all the while nodding his head. "I can convince my parents to let me keep you," the boy said happily and convincingly. "My mom and dad know how much I want to have a dog that's all my own." Jack paused for a moment to think about something important. Then he asked the male dog, "What's your name?"

"That depends." The large dog smiled at him and wagged his tail. "What do you want to call me, Jack?"

"Well," Jack said after a short pause, clearly wracking his brain for an answer to the dog's question. "You look like a stray." Jack took a moment to think some more about what to name the dog. The dog chuckled; amused by the boy's observation. "I know!" Jack said all of a sudden. He had excitement and exuberance written on his face now. "I'll call you Mutt!"

"That name suits me," the dog said and then he laughed out loud.

Mutt let out a loud bark and something magical happened to the boy. Suddenly, Jack flew up into the air, stopping just beneath the front porch awning. Mutt barked once again, and Jack began to spin in fast circles, first to the right and then to the left, stopped spinning after a moment, then touched down on the red porch!

"Wow!" Jack said loudly. He grinned from ear to ear. "That was exhilarating!" The young boy gazed at Mutt with wonder and excitement. The dog wagged his tail happily as he looked up at Jack's face.

"I like the name that you picked out for me," Mutt said with glee and amusement at the sight of the boy's hero worship. The large, shaggy dog got up from where he had been sitting on the porch, walked towards Jack, then rubbed his shaggy muzzle against Jack's hand in a friendly manner, his tail wagging from side to side. The youngster petted the dog's head with his hand and then he scratched the dog's ears. Mutt pulled his lips back and smiled at Jack. Jack felt a bond with the dog already, and he knew he was extremely lucky to have the magical pooch as his new BFF.

"Can you perform some more magic for me?" Jack asked, his awe-struck face deeply touching Mutt. The dog smiled at Jack again and nodded his head affirmatively.

"Yes, I can do that." Mutt thought for a moment, and then he said to Jack, "However, you have to do something for me first."

"Sure, Mutt." The boy looked at the dog quizzically and shoved his hands into the pockets of his blue, cotton robe. Jack shifted his weight from one foot to the other, and he wondered what it was that the dog wanted from him.

"Now, Jack, you must introduce me to your parents and convince them to let you keep me!" Mutt stared at the young boy, and Jack could tell how serious the dog was now. Jack nodded his head, agreeing with the pooch. Mutt barked once, and the front door magically opened wider and then a bunch of colorful balloons filled the front entrance.

"That was cool!" Jack exclaimed. He stared at the dog and suddenly realized that Mutt could not have opened the front door with his paw, so the dog had used magic to open the door instead. "Come inside the house, Mutt," Jack said, his voice friendly and filled with exuberance. Mutt looked into the house, his curiosity getting the best of him. Mutt walked into the front entryway of the house.

"This way," Jack said as he motioned toward the stairway that led to the second floor of the house.

The two of them climbed the staircase. They quietly made their way up to the huge, blue-and-white-striped wallpapered master bedroom and walked inside the door, which was open just enough to let the two of them enter the bedroom, where Jack's parents were still sleeping. His father and mother were both sound sleepers, and they did not hear Jack and Mutt as they made their way over to the king-size bed, which was covered with a red comforter that was pulled down from his parents' shoulders, revealing crisp, white linen sheets, and pillows. The dog and the boy could hear the man and his wife snoring loudly. Both of them snickered as they listened to the sound of Jack's parents snoring like a couple of freight trains!

"That's my Dad," Jack whispered to Mutt, for he did not want to wake his father. "His name is Howard." Mutt nodded his head, for he already knew the man's name because the dog had read the boy's mind. For the sake of introductions and to encourage Jack's good manners, Mutt pretended like he did not know the father's name. Jack motioned in the direction of his sleeping mother with his right hand. "And that's my mother." The dog nodded his head. "Her name is Martha," the boy replied.

Mutt snickered when he observed that Jack did not realize that he had been reading the 10-year-old's mind all the while. But he did so quietly so that the boy would not be embarrassed by this fact. Reading Jack's mind was an example of Mutt's magical powers, which were very impressive indeed!

Mutt thought for a moment, then said to Jack, "I have to wake up your parents now so that you can introduce me to your father and mother."

Jack nodded his head affirmatively. "Go ahead, Mutt."

The large, shaggy dog positioned himself by the left side of the bed, where Howard lay on his side, his head resting comfortably on top of a soft, down pillow. He was still snoring like a freight train.

Mutt barked once. The comforter and the top sheet both flew up into the air, then hovered in the air until they dropped down onto a blue throw rug that was lying in the middle of the hardwood floor. The dog barked again, and immediately, Howard and Martha levitated high into the air, and their eyes opened with a snap. Jack's parents were so startled by what had just happened to them that they started to tremble as they looked down at Jack and Mutt.

"What's happening?" Howard asked in a loud voice. He looked over at his wife and said, "I must be dreaming!" He pinched his arm with his fingers, and then he said, "Ouch!" Howard suddenly realized this was not a dream.

Mutt barked out loud. The married couple started spinning in circles around each other. One more bark and Jack's parents stopped abruptly. Then they started dancing together. Mutt and Jack laughed out loud as they watched the husband and his wife doing the Charleston, which Mutt caused them to do. The dog was in total control of the situation as Jack's parents continued to dance wildly together up in the air. Mutt barked one last time, and Howard and Martha suddenly separated from each other, and then they gradually descended until both of them stood on their bare feet, right in the middle of the hardwood floor.

Mutt smiled at Howard and Martha with a mischievous grin and softly chuckled. The large, shaggy, black-and-white dog observed the situation with humor. "Magic is so much fun!"

"Jack, what just happened here?" Martha asked in an incredulous voice.

"This is Mutt," Jack answered, his voice filled with exuberance. The 10-year-old looked down at the stray and grinned broadly, his eyes sparkling with a combination of awe mixed with a good dose of admiration. Mutt pulled back his lips and revealed big, white, sharp teeth. Jack then explained something important to his mother. "Mutt is a talking dog with magical powers, and he can even read my mind!" Jack looked his mother squarely in her eyes, and then he glanced at his father's mouth, which had dropped wide open. Jack continued his explanation of the situation to both his mother and his father. His parents were speechless now. "You see, Mutt is an awesome magical dog. Mutt is my BFF. And what's more, Mutt is going to help me to make some new friends who are cool and unusual!" After a brief pause, Jack looked at his parents with pleading eyes. "May I keep Mutt, Mom, and Dad? Please...this dog means the world to me!"

Howard and Martha looked at Mutt with newfound wonder and surprise. They thought about their son's heartfelt desire to have the dog as his own. Jack's parents whispered amongst themselves for a brief moment. They smiled at their only son, saying simultaneously, "Yes, Jack. You have our permission to keep Mutt." "Oh, thank you from the bottom of my heart, Mom and Dad," the 10-year-old said with an excited voice. Jack ran over to where his parents were standing in the middle of the master bedroom. He was overwhelmed with excitement and sheer joy as it dawned on him that he had just won over his parents with his explanation of his profound feelings for the stray male dog. Jack smiled at his mother without a word. The elated expression on the 10-year-old's face spoke volumes. It was clear to his parents just how much Jack loved Mutt. Jack threw his arms around his mother's waist, and he gave her a big hug. Next, Jack extended his right hand toward his father and the two of them enjoyed a moment of closeness and happiness as the youngster solemnly shook hands with his father, as if to seal the deal.

Mutt was his very own dog now!

"Now, Jack, you realize you will have to take very good care of Mutt," Howard explained in a serious tone of voice.

Father and son locked eyes.

Jack replied to his father, "I promise you that I will take exceptionally good care of my dog." The youngster was overcome with emotion, while Mutt grinned at Jack. The boy's eyes glistened as he looked at the stray. Jack owned a talking dog with magical powers that could read his thoughts!

Jack felt like he was the luckiest boy in the world.

Martha glanced down at the unkempt hound. "Well, son, you can start by giving that shaggy, matted mess of a dog a thorough, warm bath." She spoke with mock sternness, secretly amused by the burgeoning friendship developing between the boy and his prized pet. The woman smiled at her young son, her devotion and love for her only son evident in her twinkling, blue eyes. She turned and pointed in the direction of the linen closet that was located just outside the master bedroom. "You can go and get a bar of soap out of the linen closet."

Mutt let out a loud woof. Suddenly, a bar of lavender soap appeared in the palm of Jack's right hand. Jack and his parents considered the dog's magic trick with wonder and amusement. "Wow, what a cool and unusual dog you are Mutt."

"If I have to get a bath, then I'm going to smell like lavender."

Jack and his parents laughed out loud. Then, they reached out their hands to pet Mutt's matted and smelly head. The three of them smiled at the stinky mongrel. "You know, Mutt has a really good sense of humor." They thought this character trait made the pooch even more relatable and fun to hang out with. A good sense of humor made for a great BFF, especially one that was a magical dog!

Unbeknownst to Jack at the time, Mutt was allowing Jack to bathe him to teach the youngster about responsibility. It was the first of several life lessons that the magical, caring dog would teach his young master.

"Well, Mom and Dad, it's time to take Mutt outside into the backyard and give my magical dog a thorough bath in the plastic wading pool."

Mutt wagged his tail and felt a surge of love for his young master. Finally, the magical dog thought to himself, the young boy that he was mysteriously assigned to teach and go on adventures with was going to make Mutt look and smell good. Mutt realized that the simple task of Jack bathing him was an expression of love that the boy felt for his priceless BFF. The mongrel knew in his heart that his young owner would trust the magical pooch with his life and vice versa.

"See you later, Mom and Dad," Jack said in a happy tone of voice. Jack started to walk toward the door, Mutt strolling alongside him. Then Jack glanced over his shoulder, adding,

"And thank you so much for letting me keep Mutt." Mutt wagged his tail when Jack said this to his parents.

"You're welcome, son," his parents said simultaneously. They watched as their boy and his new magical BFF left the master bedroom.

Jack and Mutt walked down the staircase that was located outside of the master bedroom. Then they strolled through the spacious kitchen and stopped when they reached the back door. Jack placed his hand over the doorknob, and then he opened the back door. They looked at the backyard with unbridled happiness and anticipation. They took in the sight of the green, spacious backyard with satisfied expressions. The beautiful backyard was the envy of the neighborhood. It was replete with a large, cedar treehouse and a brand-new swing set that Jack had not used yet, but he was looking forward to trying it out with his new BFF.

Jack and his magical dog made their way over to a blue, plastic wading pool that was strategically placed so that the warm sunlight bathed it in its bright light. They glanced up at the blue sky and noted that the sun was positioned higher in the sky that was covered with white, puffy clouds. They realized then that the morning was passing by quickly. Jack watched as Mutt lay down in the soft, green grass. The magical dog said to Jack, "This grass feels so good!"

The ten-year-old smiled at the mysterious, shaggy mongrel. "Yes, you look nice and relaxed lying there like that."

Mutt read the boy's mind as the youngster now made his way over to where the green garden hose was laying in camouflage in the lush grass. The magical pooch grinned with anticipation. Now, the dog realized, the real fun was about to begin!

"I can help you with that, Jack," Mutt said as his shaggy tail wagged vigorously.

Jack glanced at Mutt, and he immediately noticed the mischievous look on the dog's face. The pooch snickered quietly. Then the dog stood up on his sturdy legs and let out a loud woof.

The blue, plastic wading pool was immediately filled with crystal-clear water.

When Jack saw that the wading pool was now filled with refreshing, cool water, he glanced from the inviting water in the pool over to where Mutt stood in the lush, green grass. Jack was amused by what his BFF had made happen with the water.

Mutt and Jack started to laugh out loud as they looked at each other. "Mutt, you can do anything that you want to with those magical powers of yours, can't you?"

"Only time will tell," Mutt replied, an air of mystery evident.

Jack wondered what his magical dog meant by that. "What do you mean?"

"You'll have to wait and see what happens," Mutt said with a mischievous look on his face.

"Okay, boy," Jack said earnestly. Whatever his pet meant, Jack knew he could trust Mutt with his life if necessary.

Mutt read the boy's mind and he smiled when he realized that Jack trusted him implicitly. The dog instinctively knew that trust was the foundation of a lasting, successful friendship.

Jack pointed at the water in the plastic wading pool, and then he said to Mutt, "Come on, get in the water."

Mutt obeyed, quickly jumping into the refreshing, clean water.

Jack splashed water over the dog's head. Then the boy wet Mutt's back and tail, his hands scooping water over the dog until Mutt's entire coat was wet. Jack thoroughly lathered up the dog with the lavender-smelling soap. "You smell better already, Mutt."

The massage of Jack's hands along Mutt's back felt wonderful to the dog.

"Oh, that feels great, Jack," the dog said with relief, happily wagging his long, bushy tail as Jack continued to give the dog a much-needed bath.

Suddenly, without warning, Mutt shook off the lavender soap from his coat. The soap flew up into the air, and Mutt snickered as the lavender soap landed all over Jack's face and torso.

"Jack, you look just like Santa Clause," Mutt said to the boy. Mutt and Jack laughed out loud. The boy just stood there, looking silly.

"Time to rinse off!"

Mutt barked once. Then the wading pool floated up into the air, and flipped over, sending a torrent of water down over both of them, removing the rest of the lavender soap from their bodies.

Jack looked down at his shirt and shorts, and in an annoyed voice, he said to his dog, "Mutt, now look at what you have done!" The ten-year-old reached up with both of his hands, and then he wiped the water from his eyes so that he could see again.

Jack turned his head in the direction of the silly dog, and then he said to him, "Mutt, what am I going to do with you?" A look of exasperation appeared on Jack's face, and he pretended to be angry with Mutt. However, Mutt read his owner's thoughts and he realized that secretly, Jack was amused by their wholesome fun!

Jack had bathed Mutt, and Mutt had bathed Jack in return.

As he looked into his dog's warm, friendly eyes, Jack grew serious as he considered Mutt for a moment. Two questions entered the boy's curious and intelligent mind. One, where did Mutt come from? And two, what kind of adventures lay ahead for Jack and his mysterious, magical dog?

Suddenly Jack understood that he was involved in a fascinating mystery, one that he'd solve more successfully with some new BFFs. Jack felt a surge of excitement. He could not wait to uncover the clues that he and his new best friends would discover together. With their help, along with the magical BFF he'd just made, Jack knew he'd successfully solve this extraordinary mystery.

Mutt read Jack's mind. A secretive smile appeared on his shaggy face. The cool, unique, magical dog knew Jack was about to embark upon an extraordinary adventure that would change their lives forever.

THE PLAYGROUND

After lunch, Jack changed into a pair of blue shorts, a red tank top, and comfortable, brown Birkenstock sandals. He laughed when he observed that Mutt had put on one of his blue and red Hawaiian shirts and tinted sunglasses. Looking Jack directly in his eyes, Mutt pulled back his lips and showed his teeth.

"Let's walk over to the school playground!" Mutt exclaimed; his voice filled with exuberance. "You can make some new friends there!"

Jack nodded his head in agreement. "That's a great idea! I can't wait to make some new friends at the playground!" The boy's eyes grew as large as saucers as he considered making some new BFFs. It'd be great to go on exciting new adventures with them. A broad grin appeared on Jack's tanned face, revealing his shiny, metal braces. Jack turned to face the full-length mirror that stood in the corner of his large bedroom. Jack pulled a tube of styling gel out of the top drawer of his chest of drawers and applied a small amount to his thick, brown hair. He put the cap back on the styling gel tube and placed it back into the chest of drawers. Jack pulled out a wide-toothed comb from his right back pocket and then he combed the gel into his unruly hair. But no matter how hard Jack tried to smooth down the back of his hair, there remained an irksome cowlick there. The cowlick made Jack look cute! Seeing this, Jack shrugged his shoulders and laughed. Mutt pointed his paw at the youngster's unruly cowlick and snickered.

Jack glanced at Mutt. "Let's go, boy!"

Mutt saw the happiness on Jack's face, but the magical dog sensed his owner was also nervous at the prospect of meeting new kids at the playground. The two of them left Jack's bedroom, walked down the stairs, and then Jack loudly announced to his parents who were still in their bedroom, "Mutt and I are going over to the school playground to make some new friends!" His parents spoke in unison when they answered him, saying, "Have a good time!"

Jack felt a wave of excitement as he inhaled deeply, steadying himself at the fantastic opportunity to make some new friends at the playground. He was beside himself with joy, and a huge grin spread across his tanned face.

The magical dog and his owner opened the white gate in the backyard, walked through it, and left the gate ajar. After walking a couple of blocks, they arrived at the playground. Mutt looked up at Jack and smiled. "Here we are, Jack."

Jack nodded his head, acknowledging what Mutt had said to him. They surveyed the playground for a moment.

Mutt had one blue eye and one black eye; he was striking to look at.

"Let's head over to the swings," Mutt said, wagging his tail happily.

They made their way over to the black, rubber swings. There were four swings. Mutt jumped up into one swing, and he began to swing back and forth, looking cool in his blue and red Hawaiian shirt and dark sunglasses. Jack sat down on the swing to the immediate right of Mutt, and soon he was swinging higher and higher into the air, moving in time to Mutt's swinging rhythm.

Mutt and Jack were having so much fun!

They soon caught the attention of a girl and a boy sitting at a picnic table. The girl's long, naturally curly blond hair and sparkling blue eyes were a marked contrast to the boy's freckled face, black hair, and intelligent brown eyes.

"Do you see what I'm seeing?" the girl asked incredulously. "That big dog is swinging on a swing!" They looked at each other, a combination of disbelief and amusement written on their faces.

The blond-haired girl and the boy with the freckles stood up from the picnic table and made their way over to the swings. They watched as Mutt and Jack were swinging back and forth on the black, rubber swings. The girl raised her right hand to her fair forehead, which blocked out the strong sunshine, so she could get a better look at the big dog on the black swing. She was stunned by what she was witnessing. The girl had never seen anything like this before in her life!

Seeing her reaction to his dog's antics, Jack slowed down his swinging, finally coming to a stop, his feet resting on the ground as he studied the girl's pretty face.

The beautiful, young girl locked eyes with Jack for a moment, and then she turned her attention back to Mutt. She could smell the lavender scent wafting from the dog's coat in the light breeze, which was gently blowing in her direction. She was surprised that the shaggy dog wearing sunglasses and a blue and red Hawaiian shirt smelled so good, fresh from a bath!

She asked in an incredulous voice, "Where did you get that dog?"

The girl made direct eye contact with Jack. Something told Jack that the girl was a real firecracker who liked getting straight to the point.

Struck by the girl's natural beauty, Jack smiled warmly at her and felt a sense of admiration for her straightforward demeanor.

"This is my buddy. His name is Mutt." Jack smiled at the girl again, and secretly wished she would become his human BFF. "Mutt just showed up out of the blue at my front door this morning. I can assure you; I was dumbfounded by our initial encounter."

"Is Mutt originally from the circus?" she asked, a puzzled expression written across her pretty, fair face.

Jack shook his head, then he said to the girl and the freckled boy who was standing beside her, "Mutt is a magical, talking dog, and he can read my mind!"

Jack grinned happily at the two of them, revealing his braces. "By the way, I'm Jack, and this is my very own dog. My parents agreed to let me keep him, and I promised them that I would take good care of my dog."

"Wow, what an incredible dog," the girl exclaimed with a mixture of wonder and a touch of envy. She wanted to have a dog like Mutt. "Do you realize how lucky you are to have a dog like Mutt?"

"Yes. I know in my heart that Mutt is going to change the course of my life."

Seeing the jealousy on the girl's face, Jack chimed in, "If you will be my friend, then I can share Mutt with you."

"Oh, wow. That is awesome, Jack." Suddenly remembering her manners, she introduced herself. "My name is Heidi." Her tone of voice changed to one of friendliness and happiness. Jack looked at his new human BFF and noticed how Heidi's pretty, blue eyes sparkled. Her positive attitude was appealing to Jack.

"Nice to meet you, Heidi," Jack said with a happy expression on his face.

Jack turned his attention to the freckled boy. "What's your name?"

"I'm Vance."

"Would you like to be my friend, Vance?" Jack asked the freckled boy, a trace of mystery and mischief evident in his voice.

"Sure, Jack," Vance said with a cheerful tone of voice. Vance stepped toward the boy with the magical dog, extended his left hand, and then he shook hands with Jack, sealing the pact of friendship with the new kid on the block.

"We'd love to have you and Mutt as our new friends!" Heidi and Vance answered simultaneously.

Mutt continued to swing back and forth as the three kids met for the first time and agreed to be friends. The dog with the magical powers looked at the kids, and as he did so, the pooch read Jack's mind. Mutt knew Jack was thinking about his new human BFFs; their meeting and becoming friends was the fulfillment of one of Jack's most fervent wishes!

What happened next was pure magic.

Mutt barked once, loudly and convincingly, and the dog's wings emerged from his shoulders. The kids gasped, then they watched Mutt, utterly spellbound, as Mutt swung as high into the air as he could. Then the dog let go of the swing; flapping his large wings as he descended to the ground. Mutt stood facing Jack, Heidi, and Vance. After Mutt pulled back his lips, revealing his teeth in a wide smile, his wings disappeared back into his shoulders.

"Wow," Jack exclaimed, "that was amazing!" Jack got up out of his swing, took a few steps toward Mutt, patted him on the head, and said to the dog, "You are such a cool, magical dog. I love what you can do with your magical powers."

"Yeah, that was incredible!" Heidi declared. Vance nodded his head in agreement.

Heidi and Vance turned to face Jack. A mischievous look appeared on both of their faces. Heidi said to Jack, "Look, we discovered a dark, mysterious cave in the forest recently."

Jack's eyes lit up. "Tell me more about the cave."

Mutt sat down, then looked from Jack's face over to Heidi's face.

"Well, don't leave me here hanging in suspense. Go on," Jack said excitedly, his eyes locked with the girl's eyes.

"You see, Jack," Heidi continued after a moment's pause, "Vance and I were too scared to go into that frightening cave by ourselves." She looked at Mutt. "But your magical dog changes everything. With Mutt, we can explore the dark cave, and Mutt's magical powers will protect us."

Jack drew a sharp breath. Heidi shifted her attention from Mutt to her new BFF, Jack.

"You two think there's something mysteriously lurking inside that cave, don't you?" Jack asked Heidi.

"You betcha," Heidi responded, her bright blue eyes sparkling with excitement and curiosity. "Jack, would you and Mutt like to go spelunking in the mysterious, dark cave with me and Vance?"

"Yes. We can find out what is lurking inside the cave," Jack answered.

"And with the help of my incredible magical powers, I can protect you kids from whatever it is that we may discover inside the cave," Mutt said convincingly. "I sense danger inside that cave," the dog added. Now the kids were even more intrigued at the thought of exploring the cave together in search of clues.

Captivated by the thought of finding some valuable clues that would help them to begin to solve this great mystery, Jack asked Heidi, "When can we go and explore the mysterious cave?" A shiver went up along Jack's spine and his eyes grew wide as he thought about going inside the dangerous cave!

"We can go to the cave early tomorrow morning," Heidi said to Jack. Her whole body trembled at the thought of what they may encounter inside the perilous cave.

However, their minds were made up. Somehow it comforted Jack, Heidi, and Vance to know that Mutt planned to use his magical powers to protect all of them once they went inside the treacherous cave. Still, they felt a twinge of fear, and they knew they would have to be very brave to follow the magical dog to wherever their adventure may lead them.

One question lingered in their minds. What would happen to them next?

THE CAVE

Mutt magically projected a map onto the forest floor from his eyes. Jack and his special dog made their way through the woods. Sunlight filtered down through the lush, green canopy. The morning was hot as they walked along, the cave being their destination. Mutt and Jack soon arrived at the dark, scary, and dangerous cave.

Heidi and Vance stood waiting at the mysterious cave's entrance. Jack and his magical dog joined their BFFs as they were gently covered with the mist wafting through the humid summer air over their bodies, and dampening their hair, from the beautiful waterfall that poured down from the cliffs that were located above the cave's entrance. Jack stepped toward the entrance of the cave so that he could peer inside the cave, but he did not see anything because it was so dark inside the musty cave.

"How are we supposed to see inside the cave when it is pitch black in there?" Jack asked Mutt. The magical pooch barked loudly, and all of a sudden, bright lanterns appeared in the three kids' hands. Jack, Heidi, and Vance suddenly remembered that anything seemed possible when they were in Mutt's protective presence.

"What about you, Mutt?" Heidi asked the dog with magical powers. "How are you going to see in the darkness when you do not have a lantern of your own?"

Mutt looked up at Heidi before answering, his lips pulled back, and revealing large, gleaming, white teeth. "Oh, you guys do not have to worry about me." The amazing dog then turned his attention from Heidi to the cave's dark, musty entrance. Mutt turned his head and looked at the three children who continued to stand outside the entrance to the mysterious, scary cave. Mutt continued to explain to the three curious and spellbound children, "I have magical eyes. That means I can see in the dark!" The incredible dog waited for a moment as what he had said to them sunk into the children's intelligent minds. "So, I will walk in front of the three of you and light the way as we make our way deeper and deeper into the interior of this terrifying cave."

"There is something inside the cave, just waiting to get us, isn't there, Mutt?" Jack asked his magical dog. When Jack asked Mutt this question, all three kids felt afraid.

"Children, the cave and whatever may be lurking deep inside of it, is part of the mystery that the three of you will have to solve. You three will just have to find out for yourselves what awaits you in the future. One thing is for certain, though, you will discover your true, brave selves today. You see, going into the cave and finding what is lurking inside is a test of your bravery."

"Follow me inside the cave," Mutt said seriously. "Walk in a straight line."

Mutt walked inside the dark, scary cave. He barked once. Two powerful beams of light came out of his eyes, just like the high beams on a car. Mutt walked deeper into the cave, with Jack following directly behind the magical dog. Heidi was second to last, and Vance brought up the rear.

Mutt's eyes illuminated the cave as they made their way towards the innermost part of the musty cave. The children held up their lanterns, so they saw clearly as they followed single file behind Mutt.

Suddenly the four of them heard scuffling sounds coming from up ahead of them. Mutt stood still, and the high beams coming from his eyes intensified in power. They saw a looming shadow that grew larger and larger on the walls of the cave as the mysterious entity closed the distance between them.

"Look!" Jack exclaimed. "It's a giant rat!"

The frightening creature had red eyes, and it was foaming at the mouth as it scuffled toward them.

Mutt barked loudly. All of a sudden, the magical dog was covered with protective quills, just like a porcupine. Simultaneously, three long, wooden spears with iron tips appeared in Jack, Heidi, and Vance's hands. Each of the three children pointed their spears in the direction of the giant, brown rat as it continued to draw nearer to them. The rat's huge, red eyes glowed menacingly. The immense rat snarled and opened its gigantic mouth, but the kids continued to watch the evil rat coming closer and closer to where they stood their ground. Mutt and the children saw the rat's tongue sticking out at them! They menacingly raised their spears when they observed the giant rat's large, gleaming teeth. The scary rat revealed its incisors, which were enormous and razor-sharp.

Mutt said in a loud voice, "Kill that huge rat, or it is going to kill us!"

The magical dog raced forward, then he moved behind the giant rat. Mutt lunged forward, and the rat's butt was covered with giant quills. The quills sticking out of the evil rat's big butt hurt like heck. Seeing this, Mutt and the children laughed out loud.

Feeling humiliated, the wicked rat walked toward the three kids in a frightening fashion. Mutt ran around to the front of the enormous creature, which bared its fangs at the magical dog. Mutt growled, and then he bared his white, gleaming teeth. The rat paused in its tracks.

Jack, Heidi, and Vance stood in front of the red-eyed rat and taunted the creature. They held their ground with determination and bravery. The three of them drew back their hands and then they threw their iron-tipped spears as hard as they could at the malevolent rat. Heidi and Vance's sharp spears lodged in the menacing rat's muzzle. The giant rat screeched in pain.

Jack's mighty spear struck the evil rat squarely between its eyes. The rat's red eyes grew dim as the creature landed on its side with a thud. Its eyes changed from red to a blank, black color.

"Hooray! The wicked rat is dead!" Mutt and the three brave children shouted gleefully and in unison. They danced around in a circle with exuberance.

A few moments passed while the four of them continued to celebrate the death of the rat that had wanted to kill them.

Mutt walked past the stinky, dead rat, followed by the three courageous kids. The four of them walked along the rock floor of the mysterious cave when suddenly, a big, glistening, metal box caught their attention. They raced towards the chest. Once they reached the large chest, they peered inside it with eyes as large as saucers. Inside the chest were many beautiful, gold coins. While Jack, Heidi, and Vance reached inside the magical chest, each of them scooping up a handful of magical, gold coins, Mutt barked once, and the sharp quills covering his body suddenly disappeared.

"We're rich!" Jack said, excitement evident in his voice. Meanwhile, Mutt grinned with satisfaction and happiness. Heidi and Vance shouted, "Hooray!"

Mutt stood there, looking into the magical chest. The golden coins gleamed in the light cast by the children's lanterns, and also by the intense beams of light coming from Mutt's eyes. The awesome dog turned his attention back to the children.

"These magical, golden coins are not for your possession, kids," Mutt explained, his voice deep and serious now.

"What do you mean?" Jack asked the dog with magical powers, his voice filled with anger. "Finders keepers!"

Mutt smiled patiently. The magical dog read Jack's mind.

"These golden coins will serve a higher purpose than just making yourselves rich."

"What higher purpose?" Jack asked quizzically.

"You kids will find out later on," Mutt answered in a mysterious voice. "Now, put your spears down, and carry the magical chest with your strong hands. Mutt looked around the cave. Then, turning his magical eyes forward, and looking in the direction of the cave's exit, Mutt commanded the children to follow him in a single file, and the children did so, carrying the magical, golden, heavy chest with their hands and holding their respective lanterns in their other hands. Looking back at the children, Mutt declared with authority, "Let's get the heck out of this terrifying cave, and move forward with the clues that await us."

Jack gulped. What clues was Mutt talking about?

THE LIVING SHIP

Excitement filled the air as Mutt, Jack, Heidi, and Vance reached the cave's exit. The children placed the golden, magical chest filled with precious coins on the floor of the cave. Looking around with awestruck eyes, they observed the red, orange, and yellow sedimentation layers that comprised the huge, rock pillars, which supported the cave's immense, breath-taking exit. A crystal-clear lake merged with the end of the cave.

All of a sudden, Mutt opened his mouth and let out a high-pitched, shrieking sound that echoed throughout the cave. The three children placed their hands over their ears in an attempt to block out the loud, jangling sound.

As the shrieking sound continued to come out of Mutt's mouth, many huge, round bubbles suddenly came up to the lake's surface. The four of them gazed into the pristine water as a large, colorful object emerged from the bottom of the lake.

"What in the world is that?" Jack asked Mutt. He felt the hair standing up on the back of his neck.

"He's the living ship," Mutt said after he had stopped making the jangling sound.

"The what?" Jack asked, dumbfounded. He took a few steps back, away from the cave's edge where it merged with the lake's surface. Heidi and Vance also stepped back, putting some distance between themselves and the mysterious, colorful creature.

"The living ship," Mutt repeated; an air of mystery around him.

The strange, huge creature fully surfaced. He looked at Mutt and the children and then blinked. He had big, blue eyes with long, black lashes. He seemed innocent enough. Jack felt a surge of courage as he returned the cute creature's gaze. Jack decided to walk toward the living ship in order to study him more closely.

Suddenly Jack realized the gigantic bubbles coming from the living ship appeared on the surface of the lake because the silly-looking, friendly, mysterious creature was breathing underwater.

The living ship was cylindrical. The creature blinked intermittently as he turned his attention to Mutt now. His eyes opened wide as he appeared to recognize Mutt. The large, shaggy, magical dog read Jack's mind. Mutt knew in his mind that Jack was wondering how the two of them knew each other.

To the living ship, however, Jack, Heidi, and Vance were strangers. The creature was very child-like, and he felt stranger danger as he looked at the three children. The living ship was also somewhat shy by nature. The living ship used his huge, colorful flippers to move backward now, putting some distance between himself and the three kids.

"It's okay. There now, boy, you don't have to be afraid of the children. They won't hurt you." Mutt pointed his paw at the closest child. The magical dog introduced the boy to the living ship with a broad smile. "This is Jack. He's ten. He's the new kid in town and he wants to be friends with you."

Jack nodded his head in agreement. He made direct eye contact with the cute creature and smiled at him warmly. After all, Mutt had it exactly right. Jack wanted to make friends with the living ship.

"Mutt, will you please introduce me to the living ship? I mean, what is his name?" Jack asked the magical dog with a look of amazement on his tanned, handsome face.

Mutt lowered his paw to the floor of the cave, then answered Jack in a friendly, happy tone of voice. The magical dog moved to the very edge of the water, and said, "This is Giggles!" Mutt looked from Giggles to Jack. The dog seemed to Jack to be in awe of Giggles, and Jack felt exactly the same way as he continued to make eye contact with the amazing, huge, colorful creature. Jack drew close to Giggles. He reached down into the water to gently pet the awesome ship's head with his hand. Jack squatted as he did so, and this enabled him to continue petting the creature's head more easily. Then Jack stood up, turning his attention to Heidi and Vance. "Go ahead and pet Giggles. He's a gentle giant."

"Can I pet Giggles?" Heidi asked, her curiosity overcoming her fear now. She turned her head and gazed at Mutt, a look of awe on her pretty face.

"Of course," Mutt answered. "Once Giggles warms up to you, you'll see that he is very friendly. Giggles loves kids!"

While Heidi petted Giggles, Vance stood in place, too awed by Giggles to do anything other than stare at the living ship. Seeing this, the living ship lived up to his name and giggled.

"Isn't Giggles great?" Jack asked Heidi as they both continued to pet the wonderful creature's head.

"He sure is!" Heidi answered, her exuberance evident in her voice.

Mutt turned his attention to Giggles. The magical dog barked loudly, and Giggles suddenly responded by opening his huge mouth. Surprised, the three kids took a few steps back. Seeing their reactions, Mutt laughed aloud.

"Come on, you guys, be brave like you all were when you killed the giant rat! Go inside the living ship!" Mutt commanded. As Mutt said this, Giggles winked at the three children. This amused the kids, causing their fear to evaporate.

Walking single file, Jack carefully made his way inside the magical, living ship's gaping, wide-open mouth. Heidi followed directly behind Jack, and Vance brought up the rear.

Giggle's tongue was pink and soft. His tongue was covered with big taste buds, which were like moguls on a ski slope. Jack continued to walk deeper inside Giggle's mouth, holding onto the magical creature's saliva-covered taste buds. Heidi and Vance followed Jack's lead, fighting to keep their footing on the slippery surface.

Next, Mutt walked inside Giggle's huge mouth. Mutt walked on his hind legs, which allowed him to grasp the living ship's slick taste buds more firmly. The magical, talking dog progressed more deeply inside Giggle's mouth, which smelled like bubble gum. Mutt's furry hind legs were covered with saliva from Giggle's mouth. It looked like the magical dog was wearing skinny jeans. Mutt reached down to stroke

Giggle's tongue, and Giggles started to purr just like a giant cat. Hearing the purring made Mutt and the children laugh. Giggles certainly was enjoying himself as Mutt continued to pet the living ship's tongue.

Jack, Heidi, and Vance continued walking deeper inside the living ship. The three children soon reached Giggle's stomach.

Mutt barked once, and the golden chest floated into Giggle's mouth. It continued to float directly behind Mutt as he reached Giggle's tonsils, which were partly living tissue and partly metal. Stopping, Mutt threw his weight against one of the tonsils. He did this for a second time. BONG! BONG! The loud sound reverberated throughout the inside of the living ship. Hearing this sound, the three kids laughed out loud.

Mutt pushed apart the tonsils and stepped into Giggle's throat. The magical dog held the tonsils open so that the gold chest could float into the living ship's throat, directly behind Mutt. The shaggy dog's head beam lights, which continued to shine from Mutt's eyes, lit up the inside of Giggle's throat.

Mutt proceeded further inside the living ship; the golden, magical chest floated directly behind the large dog. Mutt eventually reached Giggle's stomach. The magical dog barked in a commanding way, and the gold chest floated to the side of the cavernous stomach and then lowered itself to the floor of the living ship's stomach. Jack, Heidi, and Vance stood in the middle of Giggle's stomach, waiting for their canine friend. The children put their lanterns down on the living floor because the light from Mutt's eyes was more than bright enough to light up the stomach's interior.

"Hey, kids," Mutt said warmly. "I'd like you to meet a good friend of mine."

Suddenly a mysterious character stepped out into the bright light. The mystical being was a captivating, colorful wizard. He was dressed in a blue, floor-length, flowing robe, which was covered with white half-moons. On his head, the incredible wizard wore a cone-shaped hat. The wizard's hat was a deep blue color, and it had two white stripes running up along the hat's seams. The wizard was truly a sight to behold, and Jack, Heidi, and Vance stared at him, spellbound.

Jack finally managed to find his voice. "Who are you, sir?" Jack asked, his voice filled with awe and respect.

As Jack asked the question about the wizard's identity, Mutt walked over to the wizard, who reached down to scratch Mutt's long, shaggy, black ears. Mutt's coat still smelled like lavender because Jack had used the magical soap when he had given Mutt his bath.

"My name is Mr. Amazing!" the wizard finally said to the children.

"Wow, that's a really cool name!" Jack said. Heidi and Vance nodded their heads in agreement.

The three children smiled at the wizard as Mutt snuggled against Mr. Amazing's robe.

"Why have you revealed yourself to us?" Heidi asked quizzically.

"I am a pivotal figure in the mystery that you kids are trying to solve."

An air of mystery surrounded the wizard who was a master of magic.

"So, what happens next?" Jack asked Mr. Amazing.

"You'll find out," the wizard answered, his voice mysterious now. "But I guarantee what happens next is going to blow your young minds!"

THE CHAMBER OF MEMORIES

Mr. Amazing led the three children and Mutt into the magical chamber of memories. All of them felt Giggles trembling as a flashback sequence suddenly surrounded them in 3D visuals, replete with sounds and smells so intense that it made them feel like they were taking part in the memory drawn from Mr. Amazing's mind. The memory unfolded in stunning colors; a feast for the children's saucer-wide eyes.

The wizard left the chamber of memories and made his way over to the helm of the living ship, which was located in the adjacent room.

As the memory progressed, they saw a beautiful house in front of them. The children and Mutt could smell the fresh-cut grass in the backyard, and they deeply inhaled the scent with their keen noses. They enjoyed the aroma of the freshly cut grass.

The screen door beckoned Jack, Heidi, Vance, and Mutt to walk up to the house. When Jack reached the screen door, he opened it with his right hand, and then he stepped inside the kitchen, followed by the other three. The four of them walked down the main hallway, which led to the dining room.

Seated at the dining room table were a much younger Mr. Amazing and a little boy with blond hair and bright, blue eyes. It was obvious from the length of the lad's locks that he had never had a haircut.

On the dining room table, there was a birthday cake with four trick candles on top of it. The birthday cake read HAPPY BIRTHDAY AIDEN. It was a wonderfully aromatic cake, and very beautiful to look at.

"Now, make a wish and blow out your birthday candles, son," Mr. Amazing said with exuberance. Excitement filled the air.

Aiden got up on his knees on the chair and leaned forward so he was positioned above the birthday candles. He thought for a moment, his fingers resting on his small chin. Then he dropped his hands onto the top of the table, so his small hands were positioned on either side of his birthday cake as he made his wish. With a look of anticipation on his face, he inhaled deeply, and then he blew out the trick candles.

"Son, keep your birthday wish a secret so that it will come true." Mr. Amazing smiled at his son warmly and reached over to rest his hand on the little boy's shoulder. His love for his son was written across his face as he returned his hand to his side.

"I will. I promise." Aiden looked at his father with love and respect. The four-year-old revered his father and he wanted to be just like his father when he grew up.

Mr. Amazing reached for the knife and proceeded to cut the birthday cake into six slices. The trick candles remained on the top of the slices of cake.

"Father," Aiden said as he looked at the magical wizard, "can we just have some ice cream for now and open up my presents and then eat some slices of my birthday cake later on?"

Mr. Amazing looked at Aiden with surprise. "Son, you want to have some birthday cake later on tonight and open your gifts now?"

Aiden nodded his head affirmatively as he smiled at his doting father. Mr. Amazing looked lovingly at his handsome son, and it felt like his heart melted. Wanting to make his only child happy, he said to Aiden in a warm tone of voice, "Sure, son. After all, it's your birthday!"

Aiden smiled broadly as he got down from his chair and walked over to where his presents were resting in a large pile on the blue-and-white couch. Meanwhile, Mr. Amazing removed the trick candles from six of the cake slices and placed them in a small pile on top of the tablecloth that covered the dining room table.

Suddenly a huge gust of wind blew through the Chamber of Memories. Mutt, Jack, Heidi, and Vance had to brace themselves against the walls of the living chamber so that they were not swept away by the gale-force wind. Streams of vibrant colors raced past them, and they could sense the passing of time. Green, blue, yellow, orange, and red colors engulfed them in a rushing rainbow that transformed the inner walls of the Chamber of Memories into a series of color waves that moved over and past them.

Just a moment later, the gust of wind abruptly stopped. The magical ship's living walls went back to their original appearance. With their hands still pressed against the living ship's interior wall, they could feel Giggles trembling with fear.

The reason for the living ship's fear soon became evident. Moving to the middle of the Chamber of Memories, Mutt and his three friends looked around and they observed it was now nighttime.

Mutt, Jack, Heidi, and Vance now turned their attention to the trick candles, which were laying on the dining room table. One of the trick candles suddenly re-ignited. The first candle's flame quickly spread to the other five trick candles. A tablecloth lay underneath the trick candles, and it only took a few seconds for the tablecloth to catch on fire. Then the dining room table ignited into flames. After a few minutes, the entire dining room and the living room were engulfed in flames.

The wood staircase leading up to the second-floor bedrooms caught on fire next and the smoke from the fire filled the air with an acrid smell.

Mr. Amazing was reading a book in his bedroom. The roar of the flames startled him. He instinctively headed toward Aiden's room. The little boy was standing in the doorway of his bedroom. Flames threatened to engulf the blond-haired, blue-eyed four-year-old.

Aiden started screaming for his Dad.

"Father, please help me! I'm trapped!"

The fire in the hallway gained both strength and speed. Acrid, thick, black smoke coiled like a terrifying black cobra with red eyes, which forced Aiden to step backward and move deeper inside his bedroom.

Aiden yelled for his Dad. The little boy was paralyzed with fear.

"Help me, Father! Hurry! I cannot see! My bedroom is filled with smoke! I cannot breathe!"

"Hang on, son!" Mr. Amazing shouted. "I'm coming! I'll find you!"

The wizard covered his mouth with the sleeve of his robe in an attempt to stop the deadly smoke from entering his lungs. Miraculously, Mr. Amazing found the entrance to Aiden's bedroom.

"Son, where are you?"

There was no answer.

"Aiden, answer your Papa!"

Still no answer.

Frantic now and fearing the worst, Mr. Amazing got down on his hands and knees and slowly made his way over to the bedroom window. Right below the large window, which was made of stained glass, the wizard bumped into something small and soft.

"Aiden! I found you! Are you able to breathe?"

There was still no answer from the little boy.

Mr. Amazing was sweating profusely as he felt for his son's face and then he lowered his ear down until it was positioned just above Aiden's mouth. The little boy was laying on his back on the wood floor. Mr. Amazing listened carefully, but he could not hear any breath coming from his son's little mouth.

Aiden was not breathing.

Flooded with a rush of adrenaline, Mr. Amazing felt as if he had the strength of ten powerful wizards. He quickly pushed up the bedroom window so that it was almost completely open. Then, he scooped up his son in his arms and lifted Aiden through the open window, which was billowing thick, acrid smoke into the night air, and he gently lowered his strong arms, until Aiden was laying on the roof. Moving quickly, Mr. Amazing swung himself through the large window, until he was also standing on the roof.

The wizard knelt on his knees so that he was positioned by his son's chest. He began to administer CPR. He worked in a series of quick motions, trying to revive his son from the brink of death. Mr. Amazing pinched Aiden's nose closed and breathed into his son's lungs, and then he did chest compressions on the little boy.

Aiden did not respond.

Weeping now, Mr. Amazing held Aiden tight against his chest.

Aiden was dead.

How could he live without his son?

THE ANTIGRAVITY CHAMBER

Mutt and the three kids joined Mr. Amazing at the living ship's helm. There were living controls and an enormous viewscreen, which allowed them to see what was happening outside of the living ship.

"We are extremely vulnerable in the space corridor that we are traveling through now," Mr. Amazing said, his tone serious and disconcerting.

"Where are we going now?" Vance asked, puzzlement written across his freckled face. He looked nervous as he shifted his weight from one foot to the other foot.

"Yeah, what happens now?" Jack asked the wizard as he reached down to scratch Mutt's big ears.

The magical dog seemed to be quite concerned about his owner and leaned his large, shaggy body against Jack's right leg in a sincere attempt to comfort the boy.

"That's a secret," Mr. Amazing answered, his voice mysterious now. Next, the powerful wizard winked at the protective Mutt. The magical dog read Jack's mind, and he sensed the boy loved him very much, and that Jack was comforted by Mutt's concern for his owner's well-being and safety. Giggles continued to pass through the highly dangerous space corridor.

Mr. Amazing turned his full attention to the living helm. The mysterious wizard snapped his fingers and a velvety control rose from Giggle's helm. Mr. Amazing grabbed the soft, living control, then maneuvered it so that he was pulling the control backward with his right hand.

"Go faster!" the powerful wizard commanded Giggles, his voice loud and filled with authority.

Suddenly a blasting flame came out of Giggle's butt. Giggles passed gas with an audible sigh of relief. The highly combustible methane gas ignited when it hit the flame. They heard a loud BOOM, and immediately, Giggles hurtled up into the Earth's stratosphere, like a giant bat out of heck.

Mr. Amazing pushed a button on the viewscreen. The reverse view showed the beautiful, blue planet Earth getting smaller and smaller. When the Earth looked like a speck to them, Mr. Amazing pressed another large, red button on the helm of the living ship. Jack, Mutt, Heidi, and Vance noticed they were now looking at the viewscreen from a forward perspective.

Suddenly Giggles farted again. The three children, Mutt, and the mysterious wizard heard an even louder BOOM this time, then the living ship shot into hyper-speed. The shimmering stars coalesced into a dazzling array of white light that surrounded the living ship, which seemed to grow faster and stronger by absorbing the bright light around them. The magical dog, the fantastical wizard, and the three excited children turned different hues of color in vivid contrast to the blazing, white light that made hyper-speed thrilling to Giggles. Jack, Mutt, Heidi, Vance, and Mr. Amazing heard the living ship's heart beating loudly as they shot past the other planets in Earth's galaxy. Giggles settled into a smooth light speed as they hurtled past Pluto.

As Giggles continued along in the set trajectory that Mr. Amazing had typed into the living computer, which was located in the middle of the living ship's helm, Mutt read Jack's mind and said to his owner, "That's right, Jack. Mr. Amazing has something wonderful to tell you all, now that Giggles is flying right on course." Jack and the other children looked puzzled upon hearing the magical dog's words. They continued to be fascinated by the fact that Mutt could talk as well as read Jack's mind. But that was just the beginning of the mysterious and exuberant creature's magical abilities.

Mr. Amazing cleared his throat loudly, and in so doing, turned the others' attention from Mutt to himself. The magical wizard looked at them oddly, a strange combination of seriousness and yet bemusement was written on his face.

The complex, mysterious wizard said to the others, "I know watching my memory of my house fire and the subsequent loss of my son Aiden was very hard on all of you." Mr. Amazing patted his leg and Mutt sauntered over to his side. The dog with the magical powers looked up at the wonderful wizard and grinned, exposing his big, gleaming teeth. The children could not understand Mutt's sudden happy attitude. Jack, Heidi, and Vance were still feeling somber.

"Sir, I'd just like to offer my sincere condolences on the loss of your son, Aiden," Jack said to the wizard with a pained expression on his young face.

"Yes, we'd like to offer you our condolences as well," Heidi and Vance said simultaneously.

"Thank you, children, for your sympathy," Mr. Amazing replied. He sighed deeply and looked sad, tears welling up in his eyes. He had witnessed such tragedy in his younger years.

He continued, saying to the children, "There isn't a day that goes by without me feeling the hole in my heart that Aiden's demise caused me. I miss my beautiful son very much. I will never forget my son and the happiness his four young years brought to my life. He was smart and sweet, and he loved me, and I cherished him. Aiden was an extraordinary little boy."

"Yes, he certainly was a remarkable child. And his magical powers had just begun to manifest themselves," Mutt said mysteriously. The large, shaggy dog had revealed a secret, one which the three children would not come to fully understand until a later time.

Mr. Amazing paused for a moment as he gazed at Mutt and the three kids. He smiled at them, and everyone could feel the tension easing.

"But enough of that," said the wizard, who appeared to have changed his mood.

Mr. Amazing turned around and walked away from the living helm after he had shifted the living control stick into an autopilot position. Then, he motioned with his hand for the magical Mutt and the three children to follow him down a long corridor that led to an amazing chamber. The wizard stepped inside the extraordinary chamber, followed by Mutt, Jack, Heidi, and Vance.

Mutt barked once loudly and the lights inside the most excellent chamber turned on. The magical dog stood up on his hind legs and walked further inside the chamber as the three children and the wonderful wizard surveyed their new surroundings.

"This is the antigravity chamber," Mutt explained succinctly. "You guys can have fun with me inside this incredible place." He grinned from ear to ear, his lips pulled back so that his big, gleaming teeth were visible to the others.

"Cool!" Jack said exuberantly. He grinned at Mutt as Heidi and Vance stood in sheer awe of the antigravity chamber.

Mr. Amazing clapped his hands together to get the others' attention. "Well, children, I know you guys are going to have a blast in this fun-filled chamber." The wizard paused for a moment as he observed the looks of excitement and happiness that were written on the children's young faces. He continued, "As for me, I have to head back to the living helm and check out what's going on outside Giggles." And with a snap of the wizard's fingers, he vanished from sight.

Mutt barked once, and then he floated up to the ceiling of the antigravity chamber. His tail wagged from side to side as he waited impatiently for Jack, Heidi, and Vance to join him up at the top of the fantastical chamber. After the three kids looked around the interior of the chamber with saucer-like eyes, Mutt let out another loud bark, and Jack, Heidi, and Vance floated up together to the ceiling.

Mutt barked one last time and the ceiling of the antigravity chamber magically transformed into a giant trampoline. The three children clapped their hands with excitement and anticipation evident on their eager, young faces.

There were also light, thin, steel basketballs to throw into the available magnetic hoops that were located respectively at each corner of the giant trampoline. The children were upside-down, and they bounced on the trampoline.

The three kids and Mutt were having so much fun. Mutt bounced on the trampoline and then he shot a basketball into the right corner magnetic hoop. His tail wagged happily from side to side and his lips were pulled back as he looked at the children having such a good time with their furry friend.

Jack, Heidi, Vance, and the magical dog Mutt were like four ninjas with their acrobatic moves. They took turns doing upside-down flips. Then they did some upside-down flips in sync.

The three children and Mutt jumped hard on the trampoline and then they bounced to the floor of the antigravity chamber. Upbeat music came on and the walls of the antigravity chamber turned different colors. The children and Mutt pushed upwards with their feet and bounded back up to the trampoline. Mutt, Jack, Heidi, and Vance did somersaults, front flips, and acrobatic backflips.

"This is a blast!" Jack said as he did a series of somersaults, narrowly missing bumping into Heidi, Vance, and Mutt.

"Yeah, this is awesome," Heidi said with exuberance. She felt very happy now, and her emotions played across her face, which the other three observed and they felt how contagious her exuberance, love of play, and happiness were.

"I swear this is the most fun I've ever had in my life," Vance chimed in as he did several front flips and then completed a couple of backflips.

Suddenly Mutt barked loudly, just once, to get the children's attention. Weighted boots appeared on the three kids' feet. They soon found themselves standing securely on the floor of the antigravity chamber.

"Come over here," Mutt said excitedly. "There is something that I want to show you guys." The magical dog pulled his lips back, and his gleaming, huge, white teeth were observed with a great deal of respect by the three children.

The curiosity this elicited in the children was palpable inside the antigravity chamber. Mutt's owner and his BFFs clanked their way over to where Mutt stood, waiting for them. There was a hole in the wall of the living antigravity chamber, and it was covered with some kind of transparent membrane.

"What can be inside the hole?" Jack asked. He pushed his hand through the membrane, and as he did so, a bright light came shooting out from the hole that was located inside of the living wall. Jack felt the warmth of the hole as he carefully pulled out something that looked like a s'more sandwiched between two good-sized chocolate chip cookies. Jack brought the delicious concoction to his lips, opened his mouth, and took a bite of the sweet, gooey treat. A mixture of delight and pleasure appeared on his tanned face.

"Wow!" Jack said with his mouth full. Some chocolate and marshmallow drips appeared at the corners of his mouth. "It's delicious!" Jack said enthusiastically. He swallowed and then he took another bite of the delicious treat. "What is it called?" Jack asked Mutt, his voice curious.

"It's a smoogle," Mutt explained simply. "It symbolizes a mouth-watering reward for you guys' natural curiosity and bravery."

"I want to try one!" Heidi exclaimed with exuberance as she reached inside the hole in the living wall and then withdrew a smoogle with her hand. She brought the decadent confection up to her mouth and took a big bite. Her eyebrows shot up as the treat melted in her mouth. "It's exquisite!" Heidi said with a look of satisfaction.

"Hey, I want one, too!" Vance declared convincingly. He stuck out his hand with confidence and reached through the membrane-covered hole in the wall. He grabbed a smoogle and took a huge bite. Vance chewed for a few moments, and then he said enthusiastically, "Oh, this smoogle tastes so good!" He took another huge bite of the smoogle and chewed with his mouth full, closing his eyes to concentrate on the sweet taste of the magical treat. Vance concluded, "This is the most delicious dessert I have ever eaten in my life!"

Mutt did not eat a smoogle, however. The smoogles were only for Jack, Heidi, and Vance to enjoy. The treats were intended to reinforce their curiosity, but more than anything else, the smoogles were a reward for the children's bravery. Mutt knew that the three children would have to bolster their bravery and confidence to carry out their mysterious mission. Also, the smoogles had magical powers, which would enable the three children to solve the mystery that they found themselves embroiled in.

Jack, Heidi, and Vance were greatly enjoying eating their smoogles, when all of a sudden, they felt a shiver of fear running up their respective backs as if a menacing presence had suddenly entered the chamber.

The three children felt Giggles' sides moving quickly outwards and then inwards. The sound of the living ship's labored breathing only intensified the intense fear that the children felt. They sensed impending danger as the living ship shot through space and headed toward an unknown and mysterious destination.

Jack, Heidi, and Vance knew they were in imminent danger by the continued labored breathing of the living ship. They were all wondering the same thing. They thought to themselves one thing only.

What would happen next?

SPACE DRAGONS

Mr. Amazing snapped his magical fingers, and immediately, Jack, Heidi, and Vance appeared at the helm of the living ship.

Jack looked around, but someone was missing.

"Hey, where's Mutt?" Jack asked quizzically.

Mutt had extraordinarily sensitive ears. He heard Jack's question. The magical dog barked once. Mutt appeared at the helm of the living ship. He grinned at Jack, saying as he made his way over to his kid, which was what he called Jack at times, "I'm right here, kid!"

Mutt stood beside Jack. The mysterious dog flashed a smile at his owner, and simultaneously, Jack reached down and scratched Mutt's shaggy, lavender-scented ears.

Heidi looked at the wizard, a worried expression on her beautiful, young face.

"Mr. Amazing, what's going on here? Why did you summon us to Giggle's helm?" Heidi asked, her facial expression conveying her curiosity blended with a healthy fear of the unknown.

The mysterious wizard answered Heidi, his tone of voice revealing a combination of seriousness and dogged determination. Mr. Amazing peered ahead, looking through the living ship's viewscreen.

"Look! What do you see out there in space?" the wizard asked her. But his question was directed at all the children. Mutt snickered because he had figured out their situation with the aid of his magical eyes. The magical dog could already see what was out there in space awaiting them. Mutt barked loudly. Magical, telescopic lenses appeared right in front of the children's eyes, floating in the air before their faces.

Mutt sat down beside Jack and growled at the encroaching danger that was palpable in the air.

Heidi, Vance, and Jack heard Mutt growl. They felt their guts clench, and the three of them gulped loudly. They peered through their magical, floating, telescopic lenses directly into space.

The region of space that lay directly ahead of them seemed like a giant, black void. Suddenly there appeared three pairs of terrifying, menacing, red eyes. The three pairs of malevolent eyes grew larger as they drew closer to Giggles.

Heidi gasped as she took a few steps back, away from the viewscreen. The others looked at her and were shocked by the look of fear on her face.

She pointed at the viewscreen and everyone, including Mutt, turned their attention away from her to what she directed them to look at. She swallowed hard, clearly rattled and afraid of the six red eyes that peered back at her from the darkness of space. She turned and faced the others, saying loudly, "Those are space dragons!"

The three children gasped as the danger of this encounter with the three space dragons made itself abundantly clear to them. Despite their bravery in the face of danger, they all felt shivers of fear race up their spines.

The living ship was trembling, too. Giggle's huge body shook with fear. However, he was also a brave creature, and he held his ground as the three children continued to stare at the space dragons through their magical optical lenses that floated directly before their eyes. Mr. Amazing and Mutt were wondering what to do next when suddenly, all three of the space dragons spewed gigantic flames out of their scaly nostrils. Giggles instantaneously created a force field around himself that prevented the evil dragons from scorching the fantastical living ship. Seeing that they had not burned Giggles like a hog on a spit, the space dragons became enraged. They flew even closer to Giggles and positioned themselves at noon, six, and nine like the numbers found on a watch. The space dragons started to claw at the force field that surrounded the living ship. Giggles tried to escape, but the three red, scaly, evil dragons had him trapped. They began to lick their chops with their gigantic, long, scaly tongues and then they smacked their lips in anticipation.

Jack exclaimed, "Those wicked space dragons look mighty hungry!"

Mutt nodded his head in agreement. "And guess who those evil dragons are planning to have for lunch!" The red, scaly dragons with spiked tails began to take bites out of the force field that barely remained around the living ship. Giggles went to the back of the force field that surrounded him, but his evil enemies merely repositioned themselves and continued to bite holes into the membrane that was starting to disappear in chunks.

Jack spoke for all of them when he asked, "What are we going to do? Those space dragons are eating their way through Giggle's force field, and it looks like they intend to gobble us up, too!"

Suddenly a beautiful wormhole with the changing colors of a rainbow revealed herself to the beleaguered group that was trapped by the space dragons. By this time, the force field around Giggles was all but gone, enjoyed like some kind of appetizer by the enraged, evil enemies that had every intention of consuming the small group while they were still alive. The malevolent dragons started to swing their spiked tales back and forth as they broke through the remnants of the force field that had protected the small, innocent group, but no more. The children screamed in terror as they realized their demise was at hand.

One of the dangerous dragons bit Giggles on the butt. However, the three children were what the space dragons really wanted to gobble up.

"Help us!" Jack, Heidi, and Vance screamed, desperately hoping the glorious wormhole with her ever-changing colors would save the day.

"You guys seek passage through me to arrive at the parallel universe that is found on the other side of me. There, you all will discover your magical and mysterious destination awaits you."

Meanwhile, the evil space dragons rammed into Giggle's rib cage, stomach, and butt as they tried to make the living ship cough out the children into their gaping, foul-smelling mouths. The diabolical dragons fully intended to eat the children alive. The dragons were like a voracious pack of lions closing in on a wildebeest, just waiting to make the kill.

The beautiful wormhole blinked several times, revealing her lovely, blue eyes that were framed by thick, black lashes. "I will grant you passage to the other side, where the safe and secure parallel universe is waiting to protect you, children." She winked knowingly at the three youngsters. "But there's a catch!" The feminine, lovely wormhole suddenly turned a deep red color. "What's the catch?" Jack asked impatiently because he knew they did not have much time left now before each child could end up in the belly of a dragon, with hideous, horrific gastric juice enveloping each child as the respective dragon slowly digested them alive!

"Children, listen carefully to me! The three of you must prove yourselves to be brave adventurers and you guys must kill the three red, scaly, fire-breathing space dragons before I will grant you guys safe passage to the magical, mystical parallel universe in which the three of you, along with Mutt and Mr. Amazing, will find the answers to the questions you guys have been asking yourselves as you try to solve the perplexities and the mystery of this enchanting, yet perilous, adventure you have embarked upon together."

"Hurry! The space dragons are eating Giggles alive! And we know we're next in line!" Jack exclaimed loudly, then he moved away from his magical optic lenses, which continued to float in the air, right where the ten-year-old had been standing.

The evil space dragons continued to take turns biting the living ship until he was covered in blood. Giggles shrieked in agony as the three space dragons tried to eat him alive. The evil creatures, covered in scales, and with hideous, red eyes would stop at nothing to get at Jack, Heidi, and Vance.

Mutt and Mr. Amazing's powerful magic could not compare to the awesome magical powers that the beautiful wormhole, in her ever-changing colors, possessed, much like a chameleon changes its colors. The gorgeous wormhole batted her lovely eyes with their long, black lashes as she opened her mouth wide, showing the three children, Mutt, and Mr. Amazing, her inner beauty.

Mutt, however, quickly realized that he could use his magical powers to strengthen the lady wormhole's extraordinary magic. She began to pulsate, her colors changing from a cool blue and the next moment, transforming into a deep purple. She was ready to make her move! A musical cadence began to add sound to what was ordinarily silent space. Mutt matched her melodic sounds with a harmony that filled that region of space. The loud music dazed the three space dragons, who suddenly stopped biting Giggles. The beautiful sound waves washed over Giggles, and as the beautiful wormhole sang an ancient song that had been handed down through the generations of her kin, it combined with Mutt's gravelly voice to create a mesmerizing splash of music and changing colors, until Giggles was healed. Meanwhile, the space dragons started to fly around in circles, then took turns crashing into each other like three bumper cars at a county fair.

After Giggles had been restored to health, the three dragons appeared to be in some kind of a magical trance. This made them easy targets for the three children who had moved out through Giggle's mouth and appeared dressed in space armor before the three space dragons. Each of the three children wielded a long, sharp-edged, magical sword, which had one purpose only. Jack, Heidi, and Vance proceeded to take turns stabbing the space dragons in their cowardly hearts, which were cold as ice. The children knew from Mutt's telepathic communication that the dragons were hateful toward the children and only sought to kill Jack, Heidi, and Vance.

The music stopped. The battle was for the children to win. They were brave!

With a mighty plunge of their respective space swords, the three children were fighting one-on-one with the evil dragons that had tried to kill the children and gobble them up alive.

The dragons spewed forth huge plumes of flames in a futile, last-ditch attempt to kill Jack, Heidi, and Vance. But each child's space sword found its mark and the children finally killed the evil, red-eyed space dragons.

With the jet packs that they wore on their backs, the children flew back inside of Giggles, who had opened his mouth wide, allowing the children to join Mutt and Mr. Amazing at the helm of the living ship once more. Mutt barked once loudly, and the space swords disappeared. The children changed from their space armor into casual clothing, which consisted of blue jeans, T-shirts, and designer sneakers. The living wormhole could see inside the ship with her magical x-ray vision. She batted her lovely, blue eyes framed with gorgeous, black lashes as Mutt placed a gold medal around each of the children's necks.

From outside the living ship, the three children, Mutt, and Mr. Amazing heard the very lovely, lady wormhole say to the children, "I am so proud of each one of you, my young beauties. To reward your excellent bravery and because you three achieved what I had asked you to do, which was to kill the evil space dragons, I now grant you all safe passage through me so that you can finally reach the magical, mystical parallel universe that is waiting for the five of you on the other side."

Jack, Vance, and Heidi cheered as they hugged each other, and enjoyed their shining moment. The children danced around in a circle for a few moments.

Despite their happiness and excitement over having killed the evil space dragons that had intended to eat them alive like cannibals, the three children sensed that they were going to face danger once they had crossed over to the parallel universe. They puzzled over the clues that it held in store for them as they continued to solve the mystery that they found themselves embroiled in.

What clues would they find in the parallel universe? And what kind of danger would they face when they reached their destination?

PLANET ZEALON

"This magical, mystical world is called Planet Zealon," Mr. Amazing said to the children as they settled into orbit around the mysterious, beautiful, green, and blue planet. The children felt relieved to finally reach their destination after the long space voyage. "Here, in this magnificent world filled with fantastical creatures, the likes of which you can only imagine in your dreams, you will discover a series of clues that will take you guys deeper and deeper inside the mystery that is so much fun to solve. Here, too, as you three children will soon discover, all is not what it may seem!" Mr. Amazing continued to explain. Mutt nodded his head in agreement, then said to the children in a mysterious voice, "You guys cannot even begin to fathom the wonder and the mystery and the magical things that you will discover in this incredible world. Planet Zealon is unlike anything you guys have EVER experienced in your young lives. But I will reveal one important clue: this magical planet will enable the three of you to discover things about yourselves as well as the magical entities that await you guys down on the planet's surface!" Upon hearing this crucial revelation, Jack, Heidi, and Vance were overcome with a combination of wonder and exuberance!

"Well, what are we waiting for?" Mr. Amazing asked impatiently. "Let's beam down to the surface of the magical planet. Wonders galore are afoot as soon as we touch down."

"This is going to be so cool! I can't wait to discover the clues we'll find on Planet Zealon," Jack exclaimed.

"Yeah, I can't contain my excitement!" Heidi said with a look of awe on her face. She looked like she had just won the lottery.

"Well, hurry up...get us down to the surface, Mutt!" Vance said with an impatient, yet reverent expression written on his freckled face.

Mutt let out a woof. In an instant, the five of them beamed down to the surface of Planet Zealon. Jack, Heidi, and Vance looked around and immediately noticed that this beautiful, yet strange, world was the inverse of Earth. Whereas Earth had green trees and blue oceans, Planet Zealon was the opposite of Earth and it had blue trees and a green ocean.

"Wow! Planet Zealon is awesome!" Jack exclaimed.

Heidi and Vance nodded their heads in agreement. Mutt and Mr. Amazing stood off to one side, simply observing the children's reaction to their new environment. Mr. Amazing smiled and Mutt wagged his tail from side to side when they saw that Jack, Heidi, and Vance were overcome by the beauty of Planet Zealon.

Suddenly a loud GONG was heard by the five of them. The children jumped when they first heard the loud sound. They listened for a moment, then Heidi asked, "What is that sound, Mr. Amazing?" The wizard with the magical powers and Mutt seemed very relaxed and comfortable as if they had heard all this clamor before. And sure enough, Mr. Amazing knew exactly what the sound was. Mutt, for his part, also recognized the series of loud gongs and he knew exactly what it meant. However, when Mutt read Jack's mind, it suddenly dawned on him that Jack felt afraid, even though the 10-year-old put on a brave front.

"Those gongs are coming from the capital city, which is called Xethen." Mr. Amazing raised one hand and stroked his long, white beard with his fingers as he contemplated what they should do next. Mutt, who now sat down next to his friend, the wizard, looked at Jack, Heidi, and Vance with a mysterious expression.

Mr. Amazing snapped his fingers and a globe made of pure crystal appeared. The magical wizard, accompanied by Mutt, sauntered over to the magical object, which had a hazy fog swirling inside of it. The mysterious orb floated in the air as the magical wizard grinned from ear to ear and seemed pleased to have made the fog-filled object materialize right in front of them. Only a powerful wizard who possessed years of expertise in the practice of this kind of special magic was capable of such an accomplishment.

"I can see what is happening in the capital city as I gaze into the magic ball," Mr. Amazing explained to the three kids who now moved towards the mysterious object and then they stood in a circle around the mist-filled, crystal globe.

"In real-time?" Jack asked, his voice filled with hungry curiosity, one that the other two children shared.

"Yes," Mr. Amazing said in response to the curious 10-year-old's question.

Mutt barked loudly, and suddenly, the misty vapor inside the crystal globe vanished, and the children saw what was happening in Xethen.

They saw a feast that was filled with happy, laughing Zealonites. They were celebrating an enormously important event because they wore different colored, velvet tunics with gold fringe. Not only did the celebrants wear gorgeous dress outfits, but they were extremely beautiful creatures that used their magical powers to lift the food or the drink that they desired to consume into the air and float it over to where they sat at the beautiful table with its splendid grain of wood. The Zealonites were sitting around an immense, long table made from a kind of wood that the kids realized was not found on Earth. Happiness filled Jack, Heidi, and Vance's hearts as they carefully watched the merriment taking place right in front of their eyes. The three children soon discovered that they had magical vision. Whenever they wanted to see something more in detail, the three kids just had to focus their attention and they saw whatever they wanted to observe in greater detail. Afterward, when the children had studied some aspects of the celebrating Zealonites closely with their respective magical vision, all they had to do was relax and their vision returned to normal.

The children soon discovered the partying Zealonites had a great sense of humor. One of the beings dropped the bottle of whatever mysterious concoction he wanted to drink and another Zealonite sitting next to him transported a delicious-looking cake right up to the creature who had dropped his drink and smashed the big cake into the poor creature's face. Seeing this, all the other Zealonites erupted into laughter. This comedic action struck Jack, Heidi, and Vance as hilarious, and they shared a good belly laugh with each other. Mutt and Mr. Amazing, for their part, looked amused and clapped their hands and paws together with delight.

After his belly laugh had quieted down to just giggles, Jack asked Mutt and Mr. Amazing a very important question. Happiness and curiosity mixed in the expression on his face. "What are the Zealonites celebrating?" Jack asked, no longer afraid, but instead feeling an intense curiosity about what he was witnessing right before his very eyes.

Mutt smiled at his kid as the magical wizard answered Jack's extremely important question. Mr. Amazing made intense eye contact with Jack.

"My fellow Zealonites are celebrating the Festival of the Heart Tree."

"What's that?" Jack asked with a perplexed expression on his handsome, tanned, innocent face.

Heidi and Vance looked at each other in confusion.

The three children had never heard of The Festival of the Heart Tree. They suddenly felt as if they were very far from home. Nothing like this celebration ever happened on Earth!

"Well, why don't we travel across the blue jungle to Xethen, and then you can see for yourselves what the Festival of the Heart Tree is." As he spoke to the children, Mr. Amazing winked at them. "That way, you can discover more clues to the mystery that you are trying to solve."

Suddenly Mutt lay down on the soft ground. The magical dog was exhausted by the long space voyage they had taken through the parallel universe to reach Planet Zealon.

Worried by the sight of his canine BFF laying on his side and panting even though the temperature was perfectly comfortable and there was no humidity, Jack felt a deep sense of compassion towards the poor exhausted dog. "What's wrong with Mutt?" Jack asked, his unusually high voice revealing the intense anxiety that he was feeling.

Mutt read Jack's mind, and sensing his owner's distress, spoke just above a whisper, saying, "Jack, I have to get to the Heart Tree and its magical fruit. My magical powers are ebbing and only the heart fruit can restore me to normal. Please help me to get to the Heart Tree right away."

Jack looked directly into Mr. Amazing's green eyes. Then he asked the ancient wizard, "Do you know of some kind of magic that can take us to the Heart Tree so I can help Mutt to return to health?" The magical wizard noticed Jack had made his way over to Mutt and after bending down, the boy was petting his dog's head.

Having lived in Iceberg, Minnesota for a long time, Mr. Amazing declared in a loud voice that was filled with authority, "You betcha!"

Mr. Amazing cast a spell on the crystal globe, and immediately, something akin to a large, hot air balloon appeared right before their very eyes. Seeing this, Jack was flooded with relief. "Oh, thank goodness!" he said to Mr. Amazing.

On the surface of things, it seemed to the five of them that everything was going to be fine now that they had the flying hot air balloon to take them straight away to Xethen.

However, they weren't safe until they reached the magical Heart Tree's protective force field. Knowing this by the telepathic communication that was taking place between Mr. Amazing and Mutt, so as not to frighten the children, Mutt did not tell the children that they were in grave danger.

They took turns getting into the hot air balloon that was covered in colorful feathers. Jack carried Mutt over to the balloon and carefully placed him in the skin-covered basket. When Jack grasped the top of the basket and looked up to see the feather-covered balloon gently lift off from the ground, he realized that the hot air balloon was a living entity. Another kind of living ship!

The living hot air balloon, even though it was an airhead, somehow managed to plot the course that would take all of them to the capital city.

Mutt and Mr. Amazing gazed into each other's eyes and nodded their heads in telepathic agreement.

The hot air balloon would be sailing right over the blue jungle until it reached the periphery of the jungle. The fantastical creatures in the blue jungle posed a direct threat to stopping them from reaching the Heart Tree and the magical heart fruit from the Heart Tree that Mutt needed so desperately. Without the magical heart fruit, Mutt would die.

Mr. Amazing realized there was only one thing that he could do with his powerful magic. But he was ancient, and it had been a long time since he had used that kind of magical spell against the jungle's inhabitants that were so intent on meddling with their extraordinary adventure.

Would Mr. Amazing's magical spell be powerful enough to thwart the fantastical creatures in the blue jungle from destroying the five of them as they flew towards the capital city, and discover more about the Heart Tree that grew in the middle of Xethen?

THE HEART TREE

Luckily, Mr. Amazing's powerful spell had saved the day. He had carefully spoken the words to the spell and the living hot air balloon had become invisible. They had safely made their way across the top of the canopy of the blue jungle. They softly landed on the ground at the center of Xethen.

They got out of the skin-covered basket and made their way over to the huge, iron gate that protected the Heart Tree. A high, stone wall surrounded the beautiful, magical tree that bore the heart fruit that Mutt needed to eat in order to live. Jack pushed hard against the gate, but it would not budge.

The Heart Tree looked at Jack with his eyes that were in the front of his massive, purple trunk. He was very different from the other trees they had seen as they had flown over the top of the blue jungle. The Heart Tree's trunk and branches were not blue. At first, they were purple, but then they began to change colors like a chameleon. This kaleidoscope of colors was not the only thing that made the Heart Tree different from all the other trees on Planet Zealon. Since he had a mouth, the Heart Tree could talk!

"Not so fast, Jack," the Heart Tree said to the boy as he continued to try to open the iron gate, leaning his full weight against the green gate. "There is a clue to be discovered first."

Upon hearing this revelation, Jack stopped pushing against the green gate as he made direct eye contact with the Heart Tree's blue eyes. The emotions he saw in those eyes deeply moved him. Jack instinctively understood that the Heart Tree wanted to save Mutt's life, but there was a price that must be paid first.

"What clue are you talking about?" Jack asked impatiently, for he knew Mutt was close to death and suffering.

"Look deeply into my eyes, Jack. What do you see?" the Heart Tree asked.

Jack focused on the Heart Tree's big, blue eyes. "I see the golden chest that we brought inside of Giggles after we had slain the huge, evil rat that had been hiding the chest, and had intended to keep the treasure all to itself."

"I want that golden chest and the gold coins it contains in exchange for me allowing Mutt to eat some of my heart fruit. My heart fruit is very precious, and I seldom share the heart fruit with someone else. However, if you can find a way to transport the gold coins inside the golden chest to me here, I will make an exception. You get the treasure for me, and the green, iron gate will open for you, thereby allowing Mutt to eat some of my heart fruit, which as you know, is the only way to save your beloved dog's life." The Heart Tree continued to stare at Jack with his eyes filled with anticipation.

Jack realized this was the clue that the Heart Tree spoke of earlier. Jack looked over at Mr. Amazing as Mutt read Jack's mind. Though in a weakened state, Mutt still experienced the bravery and dogged determination of his kid. This determination moved Mutt deeply as he realized Jack would do anything to help him. Mustering his courage and with the last ounce of strength he had, Mutt willed himself to stand up and move towards Jack, until he was standing right beside his human BFF.

"You have a deal!" Jack exclaimed, and he felt happiness and comfort as he realized Mutt was not going to die after all.

"Can I do anything to help you, Jack?" Heidi asked, her compassion for Mutt filled her heart with a deep yearning to save Mutt's life, too.

"Thank you, Heidi. Your affection for Mutt is obvious to all of us." Jack thought hard about the situation, then he concluded by saying to her, "However, this is between the Heart Tree and me. I'm Mutt's owner, and so, it's my responsibility to do as the Heart Tree has asked. I have to find a way to get the golden chest that's filled with those precious, gold coins and give the gift of gold to the sacred tree so that Mutt can be saved by eating some of the magical heart fruit."

Jack looked over at Mr. Amazing, and when their eyes met, the magical wizard could see that the 10-year-old was pleading for his help.

Mr. Amazing decided to check with Mutt first before he answered the boy's fervent plea for help. The magical wizard spoke to Mutt telepathically. The dog answered yes, also by telepathic communication.

Mr. Amazing shifted his attention back to Jack, who was still staring at him.

"Yes, I'll help you to get the golden chest filled with its gold coins in order to pay the Heart Tree." The magical wizard pulled out a papyrus scroll from the inside of his pocket, and then he began to read aloud the sacred text that was written in the ancient scroll, which he had obtained from the Egyptian king, Tutankhamun, in a trade they had made eons ago.

As soon as he had finished reading the text from the magical scroll, Mr. Amazing started to dance in circles, and Jack, Heidi, and Vance soon joined in the merriment. Everyone felt delighted because they knew that after Mr. Amazing gave the golden chest with the gold coins inside it, the Heart Tree would proceed to heal their BFF, Mutt.

The group continued to dance and then they began to sing together as the power of the magical scroll started to kick in.

The wind began to howl and blew in great gusts. As soon as they witnessed this, Mr. Amazing, Jack, Heidi, and Vance stopped dancing and singing. The group watched as a brilliant white light erupted from the ground, which split open.

Suddenly they saw the golden chest rise from the giant fissure in the ground.

"Where did the golden chest come from?" Jack asked in bewilderment.

"Yeah, that's what I was about to ask," Heidi said as she watched the magical chest filled with its precious coins floating through the air towards the Heart Tree. The incredible chest rose just high enough that it cleared the green, iron gate and then it slowly descended to a spot on the ground that the Heart Tree had illuminated.

"I thought the golden chest was still inside Giggles," Vance pointed out.

"It was. However, Giggles is having a day at the spa. He is being spoiled rotten by some beautiful mermaids. The lovely mermaids are giving the living ship a facial and they are also going to give Giggles an all-body massage. Giggles is so relaxed that when he yawned, the chest simply floated out from the living ship's enormous mouth, and the chant I spoke from the sacred scroll caused the ground to split open. Then the magical chest came to rest on the spot on the ground that the Heart Tree designated," Mr. Amazing explained in detail.

Suddenly they heard Mutt whining. The dog with the magical powers could not use his magic to save himself from the suffering that he was being forced to endure as the wizard talked about such things as Giggles enjoying a spa day. Listening to the story only served to increase the poor dog's pain and distress. Mutt sat down and his head drooped and then his large, pink tongue moved in and out of his mouth. When Jack saw that his BFF was starting to foam at the mouth and there was some blood in Mutt's drool, Jack freaked out. For their part, Vance, Heidi, and Mr. Amazing glanced at the large, scruffy dog that still smelled like lavender from his bath some time ago, and they grew very concerned about the state that Mutt was in.

"All right, darn it, that's enough of this crap," Jack said with anger, his lips snarling at the corners of his mouth. "We gave you the magical chest filled with its precious, gold coins. Make good on your promise Mr. Heart Tree and heal Mutt. Just look at the poor dog. He's on his death bed!"

"It's true. You gave me what I wanted, and now, I'm going to give you what you want, my brave child." The mystical, magical Heart Tree looked down at Mutt, and he felt compassion for the poor creature. The enormous tree, which was bejeweled with his colorful heart fruit, knew he had to do something immediately or else the pitiful, suffering Mutt would die.

Tension filled the air.

"I'm going to save your life, Mutt," the Heart Tree declared as a gentle, refreshing breeze rustled his leaves. The poor dog felt the cooling breeze descend upon him and he closed his eyes with relief.

What happened next astounded all of them. Even the Heart Tree seemed amazed by the powerful magic that he displayed for all to see. The sacred tree's kaleidoscope-like trunk and branches suddenly broke into a brilliant white light. The Heart Tree reached up with one of his branches and pushed his heart fruit up and down at his crown, showing off his magical fruit, which no other tree possessed throughout the entire universe.

The gorgeous, white, healing light enveloped Mutt. It took a moment, but soon, the panting dog stopped foaming at the mouth and there was no longer any sign of blood in his drool.

"Rise, Mutt!" the Heart Tree commanded the dog. "Eat my magical heart fruit so that you may be completely healed. The best heart fruit is up at the top of my branches!"

Suddenly Mutt felt just enough strength to display his feathered wings, which appeared from his shoulders. With a mighty beating of his wings, Mutt flew up to the top of the Heart Tree. He grabbed a piece of the heart fruit, then swallowed. As he did so, the magical dog felt a deep sense of gratitude.

As Mutt continued to take partake of the life-saving heart fruit, he turned from black-and-white into a blinding shade of white. Down on the ground, Jack and the others had to look away because the brilliant, magnificent, white light hurt their eyes.

The Heart Tree shouted in the air, and immediately, sunglasses appeared on the faces of the witnesses to this series of wonderful events.

Looking up at Mutt again, Jack, Heidi, Vance, and Mr. Amazing saw the magical dog was sound asleep and nestled amongst the soft leaves at the top of the Heart Tree. The magical tree turned a comforting shade of green and softly sang a lullaby to Mutt.

Mutt was healthier now than he had ever been before in his life. The gentle, refreshing breeze was comforting to the sleeping dog and his loyal, brave BFFs that continued to stand on the ground, and all of them felt a deep sense of peace and well-being as they continued to watch Mutt sleeping up at the top of the Heart Tree.

"Come closer to me so that I might look upon all of you," the Heart Tree said in a gentle tone of voice. He beckoned them over with a wave of one of his branches.

"Remove your sunglasses so that you guys can look at me while I give you some critical instructions to follow."

Jack, Heidi, Vance, and Mr. Amazing did as the Heart Tree commanded. They took turns taking off their respective sunglasses as they made their way over to the awe-inspiring Heart Tree.

Mr. Amazing reached inside the right pocket of his robe, and he twirled the lock of his son's blond hair that he always carried with him. He turned the lock of Aiden's hair around and around with his fingers. This helped him to remember his little boy who had died from smoke inhalation when their house caught on fire, filling the air with plumes of smoke that had cost his four-year-old his brief, precious life. Tears appeared in his eyes as he remembered happier times when he had taken his son fishing, on hikes, and swimming during the summers they had shared as father and son. What he would give to get his little boy back again!

The Heart Tree addressed them in a serious tone of voice. "I want you to fly over the top of the town square and then follow the road that will lead you guys to the Center for Lost Children. When you guys arrive at the Center, a small group of brilliant medical researchers will greet you. They are waiting for you at this very moment."

Upon hearing this, Mr. Amazing clutched his little boy's lock of hair in his hand. The magical wizard had a sense of why their small group would have to take the living hot air balloon so they could go over to meet the scientists who waited for them to arrive at the Center for Lost Children.

Jack, Heidi, and Vance surmised they would find more clues at the Center, which would enable them to delve deeper into the mystery they so fervently wanted to solve. They guessed correctly that they had been brought to Planet Zealon by Mr. Amazing for an important reason. One critical question kept crossing their young, curious minds.

Why was the mystery they embarked upon taking them to the Center for Lost Children?

THE CENTER FOR LOST CHILDREN

Jack, Heidi, Vance, Mutt, and Mr. Amazing flew to the Center for Lost Children in the living hot air balloon, which had feathers covering the balloon and a warm, skin-covered basket.

When the group of adventurers reached their magical destination, they climbed out of the basket and then made their way up the flight of stairs to the front door of the Center. The five of them soon discovered the magical door had brown eyes and that the front door could speak to them.

Jack reached over with his hand and turned the doorknob, but the front door wouldn't open.

"Let us in, Mr. Door. We are here on important business. There are important clues to be discovered inside the Center that we need to figure out to solve the mystery in which we are involved." Feeling frustrated, Jack added, "Please tell me how to open you!"

Mutt explained to Jack, "He's an obstinate door because he guards the Center for Lost Children. He prevents unwanted creatures from getting inside this place. Only I know how to open the front door to the building."

The others watched as Mutt opened his magical mouth. He projected a secret code onto the door. Then he spoke to Jack by telepathic communication. The message was only for Jack. The rest of the group remained in the dark as to what would happen next.

Jack saw a keyboard appear on the right side of Mr. Door. The 10-year-old punched the secret code into the keyboard, and as soon as he did this, the front door changed from red to green. Jack turned the doorknob, and this time, Mr. Door swung open. The front door also had a mouth and he smiled at Jack and the rest of the group.

"Welcome, my friends, to The Center for Lost Children. What you guys seek to find in terms of the clues you need to continue solving the mystery will be revealed to you here," said Mr. Door. As Mutt closed his mouth, Mr. Door smiled again at the three children, the powerful wizard, and the magical dog.

The five of them entered the magical room and they saw the three medical scientists that were waiting for them off to one side of the huge, white, clean room. Everything inside the place was white, from the floor to the walls and the ceiling. The room was perfectly comfortable even though no thermostat was in sight. The room was a living creature and it communicated by telepathy with the kids, Mutt, and Mr. Amazing.

The living creature spoke to the medical scientists in a normal way, however.

"You must help Mr. Amazing and his wondrous friends."

The three scientists said simultaneously, "We will help the powerful wizard now. Follow us over to the incubator that's located on the other side of the room."

Mr. Amazing and his four friends did as they were instructed. The three medical scientists led the way, with the group of guests following behind them. As the group made their way over to the small, blue-and-white incubator that was located right next to the far wall, they observed all the technological marvels inside the living room. They noticed the buttons, levers, and machines inside The Center for Lost Children. The five guests reached a logical conclusion as they finally arrived at the small incubator and then stood around it in a circle, holding hands. They felt confident that something magical and mysterious was about to happen.

The three medical scientists spoke in unison, saying to their guests, "We are going to proceed now, friends. Watch as the magic unfolds before your very eyes!"

Dr. Markham was the senior medical doctor. He sure didn't look like a doctor! He was fat and his blue shirttail was hanging down from the back of his pants. Not only that, but he also had some chewing tobacco that magically disappeared whenever he spat a piece of the chaw out of his mouth. He wasn't the healthiest doctor, but he knew exactly what he was doing after he'd completed so many years of medical school and then he'd successfully completed his Ph.D. in Zealonite anatomy and physiology. His medical colleagues were Dr. Beecher and Dr. Olson. They were identical twins, the very epitome of excellent health.

Dr. Markham walked over to where Mr. Amazing stood, his hand in his pocket. Mutt knew from telepathic communication with the ancient wizard what he had in the pocket of his flowing robe. However, Jack, Heidi, and Vance were in the dark.

"Please give me the thing you know I need to complete my work."

"Of course, I'll hand it over to you right now," Mr. Amazing said with excitement. The magical and powerful wizard withdrew a lock of Aiden's blond hair and gave it to Dr. Markham. The senior doctor blew on the blond hair for good luck. That's what Zealonites did when they wanted an excellent outcome!

Meanwhile, Dr. Olson and Dr. Beecher were finagling with a big machine that had all kinds of buttons, levers, and switches on the front of it. Dr. Markham sauntered over to where his colleagues were entering a series of codes into the sophisticated, gleaming machine. "Be careful to double-check the sequencing that you are entering into the powerful machine," the senior medical doctor said to his colleagues, who were also close friends of his. "Of course, my main man. I guarantee you the sequencing will yield an excellent result." The identical twins always spoke together when they were in a serious conversation with their BFF, Dr. Markham. As the twin medical doctors said this to Dr. Markham, Jack, Heidi, and Vance noticed their pupils widened and then changed into dime-sized, red hearts, which revealed the love that they felt for each other! After a moment of their visual exchange of love, the three doctors gave each other a thumb's up. Mr. Amazing smiled when he saw their pupils change into small, red hearts. As the powerful wizard turned his attention to the lock of blond hair that stuck out on either end of Dr. Markham's clenched fist, the magical wizard's pupils turned into red hearts, revealing the love that he felt for his son, Aiden. Next, the doctors and Mr. Amazing turned their attention back to the task at hand. The wizard and the three medical doctors listened to the big machine humming as the lock of Aiden's hair went into a slot located in the front of the magical machine. While this was going on, their pupils reverted to normal.

By this time, the children had grown weary of simply watching the events unfolding before their very eyes in silence, and Jack decided to speak up for their small group of three. Reading Jack's mind, Mutt sensed the exasperation Jack felt at that moment.

"Will you please tell me and my BFFs what the heck is going on here?" Jack shoved his hands deep inside his pockets. As the leader of the group of children, Jack was brave, and he didn't hesitate to speak his mind when he was upset. "After all, you have dragged me and my dear friends halfway across the universe to Planet Zealon. After that long journey through space on the living ship, I'd say we've earned the right to know what you guys are doing!" Simultaneously, Vance and Heidi crossed their arms; they were not going to wait anymore for an explanation from the three medical doctors. Mutt saw how defiant and brave the children were as they waited impatiently for some kind of explanation as to what was going on, and the friendly dog smiled at them with pride written on his shaggy, black-and-white face. "Yeah, you guys may be brilliant scientists, but you sure are secretive! The children want to know what you are doing with that lock of Aiden's hair that you put into this humming machine! So, tell them, what's going on here, doctors?" Mutt locked eyes with Dr. Markham because he was the smartest and the most experienced of the three medical doctors.

Dr. Markham looked from Mutt to Jack. "We're not purposely being secretive about this situation. Nothing like this experiment has ever been done before at The Center for Lost Children. Surely, however, you guys must realize the name of this living building is a clue that will help you to solve at least some aspects of the mystery. Put on your thinking caps, my dear children." The senior medical doctor smiled at the three children encouragingly.

Suddenly a kind of gloppy material appeared from the humming machine and flowed down the long tube that was attached to the blue-and-white incubator that they were standing around. The gelatinous goop began to accumulate inside the incubator, but it was without form or shape yet.

"OOOH," Jack exclaimed in a loud voice.

"That stuff looks gross!" Heidi declared.

A strong odor came from the incubator. Pinching his nose with his fingers, Vance said, "Geez, that crap really stinks!"

Everyone laughed when Vance said that.

The three kids and Mutt moved closer to the incubator and peered inside it to get a better look at what was going on. They all looked shocked as the goop slowly took form. First, legs formed right in front of their eyes. Then the trunk took shape, followed by shoulders and arms. The last thing to transform from the gelatinous material was a beautiful face of a four-year-old boy. The little boy had sparkling, blue eyes, and semi-long, shiny, blond hair. His cheeks were ruddy, and he seemed to be the perfect picture of good health.

"Aiden!" everyone exclaimed simultaneously. They stared at the little boy; they were all in shock!

"My son is alive again!" Mr. Amazing shouted as tears of joy ran down his cheeks.

Jack looked perplexed. "But how can that be?! We saw Aiden die from smoke inhalation during the terrifying fire that burned down your house!"

"Yeah, I don't understand how Aiden can be alive again. Is this a clone?" Vance stared at Aiden as he tried to make sense of what had just happened.

"It's a mystery," Heidi concluded. She didn't understand yet what had truly happened.

"Aiden is alive, and he is not a clone," Dr. Markham explained to the others. "You see, children, we took some DNA from the lock of hair that was placed inside of the machine and then the magical, humming machine sequenced the DNA so that the goop you all saw was transformed into Mr. Amazing's son." He paused for a moment and then he said, "Aiden has been reanimated!"

"Reanimated?" Jack asked, clearly puzzled by a term he had never heard of before. "What exactly does that mean?"

"Simply put, reanimation is a process whereby a lost child can be brought back to life after his DNA has been properly sequenced by the magical, mysterious machine. However, that's just a theory of mine. You must understand, children and Mutt, that not even medical doctors have all the answers. Only the mysterious machine knows exactly what just happened with Aiden. The machine has magical powers, and he puts that magic to good use here at The Center for Lost Children!"

"Yes, he's right! Only the living machine knows exactly what happens during the reanimation process!" Again, the identical twin doctors had spoken simultaneously.

"I see," Jack replied. "So, what happens to Aiden now? I mean, why is he here? Why is he alive again?"

"I am the king of Planet Zealon," Mr. Amazing revealed to the others. "But I have grown old on Earth. I am not capable of fulfilling my duties as king of my world any longer. Aiden is heir to the throne. My son will be Planet Zealon's next king. Also, he will grow up to be the most powerful wizard in the universe. He will receive his magical powers by eating some of the heart fruit that the Heart Tree grows. All I know as his father is that Aiden has a mission to complete, and it's an important one. Something that has to do with Earth. You see, I had a dream about my son, and in the dream, I saw Aiden sitting on the throne, surrounded by all kinds of fantastical creatures. But a loud noise jarred me from my sleep, and I did not get to see how the dream ends."

The children looked shocked upon hearing this revelation from Mr. Amazing.

Jack felt as though he was in a dream. But he was tired, and he could see from the sleepy looks on the faces of his friends that they were exhausted, too. After all, the only one who had gotten any sleep in the last few days was Mutt, lucky dog!

"Where are we going to stay tonight?" Jack asked wearily.

"There is no night on Planet Zealon," Mr. Amazing explained. He felt compassion for the exhausted, brave children and he decided to help them sleep. Poor things!

"We are so tired, Mr. Amazing," Heidi replied.

"Yeah, all I want to do now is sleep," Vance added.

"I know, children. You must rest or you will get sick. You fragile humans! When I am on Planet Zealon, I never have to sleep. I'll be awake for the rest of my life. I drink a magical, caffeinated beverage that enables me to always stay awake."

"You mean to say Zealonites drink coffee?" Jack asked, clearly amused. He and the other children laughed out loud.

"Well, we drink something like coffee. But the beverage that I consume is considered a delicacy on Planet Zealon. The drink comes from a native plant that only grows in the blue jungle. I have loyal spies that sneak into the blue jungle so that they can bring the magical plant's leaves home to me, and then they brew the concoction that in my opinion, only a king should drink. But my subjects are not as loyal as my spies, who are knights, and as a result, the magical plant's leaves are sold on the black market, and they fetch a handsome price."

Mr. Amazing knew it was time for them to leave The Center for Lost Children and go home to his castle that was floating in the clouds just outside Xethen. But before they left the Center, the powerful wizard had to remove Aiden from the incubator and get him dressed in some warm clothes. Mr. Amazing opened the top of the blue-and-white incubator and then he took his son into his arms. "You'll be safe with me now."

"Daddy! Is it really you? Have you come here so that you can take me home to your castle? I can't remember for sure, but I think our house on Earth burned to the ground! Please take me home to your castle, which is made from stones, so that I never have to go through that nightmare again!"

"That's exactly what I'm going to do, my precious son. You are safe with me. My magical powers are much stronger on Planet Zealon than they ever were on Earth."

"Oh, that's good to hear!" Aiden smiled at his father and Mr. Amazing squeezed his little boy with his arms. The magical wizard knew that his son would never need to sleep, which was in sharp contrast to Jack, Heidi, and Vance. Earthlings were so fragile; it seemed like the children from Earth needed to crash at the castle or they would just collapse from sheer exhaustion.

Mr. Amazing held Aiden in his arms as he looked at the small screen that suddenly appeared in the palm of his hand. He observed Giggles swimming happily in the gigantic moat that surrounded his castle. He breathed a sigh of relief as he sent a telepathic message to the living ship. Giggles looked content after his day at the spa with the beautiful mermaids that had given the living ship a facial and a full-body massage. Giggles had deserved a spa day! After all, the living ship had safely flown them halfway across the universe to the magical Planet Zealon. Giggles had brought him home to his son, Aiden, and for that, Mr. Amazing felt profoundly grateful.

The magical wizard gathered together the three children and their BFF, Mutt. He marveled at the gift of friendship they shared. They had bonded and were close friends after all that they had been through together. Looking into Jack's drooping eyes, the wizard sensed the relief from the loneliness that his BFFs had brought into his young life.

"C'mon everybody, it's time to go home now," Mr. Amazing said happily.

The three kids, Mutt, Mr. Amazing, and Aiden left the Center and got into the living hot air balloon. They sailed up into the clouds, where the floating castle was located. When they reached their destination, they got out of the hot air balloon, then made their way over to the castle's gigantic moat, where the very relaxed Giggles greeted them warmly. Giggles had enjoyed his day at the spa and being pampered by the beautiful mermaids, who had waited on him hand and foot. However, the living ship had missed his friends and he was happy to see them arrive home safely. Giggles acted like a watchdog, keeping the children, Mutt, Mr. Amazing, and Aiden safe inside the floating castle.

"There, sleepy heads, time to get a good sleep." Mr. Amazing had not said 'get a good night's sleep,' for there was never nighttime on Planet Zealon. The powerful wizard put the three kids to bed, and then he reclined to the large stateroom that was located deep inside the floating castle, his son safe and sound in his arms.

"How would you like to hear a good story?" Mr. Amazing asked Aiden.

"Oh, father, I would love it if you would tell me an exciting story, one that's filled with excitement and adventure!"

Mr. Amazing knew that his mysterious story could not be too long, for the wizard had been called to the Council of Elders, where as king, he was at the top of the list of distinguished Zealonites and visitors from Earth. They had a critical discussion before them, but as the leader of the Council, the king of Planet Zealon must make sure they arrived at a plausible solution to the problem they were facing. Jack, Heidi, Vance, and Mutt would be coming with him. However, Aiden would stay at the floating castle, where Giggles would babysit the little boy. Mr. Amazing knew Aiden would be safe with Giggles, who would lay down his life, if need be, for the king's son, and protect the heir to the throne!

The Council of Elders must be ready to address the challenge they faced. However, their solution remained a mystery, one that the Earth children had to solve. The clues were right before their eyes, but would Jack, Heidi, and Vance be able to finally get to the bottom of the mystery they needed to solve?

Only time would tell. However, Mr. Amazing knew one thing was for certain. The Earth children's bravery would be tested once again!

Were Jack, Heidi, and Vance up to the challenge?

THE COUNCIL OF ELDERS

The living hot air balloon was exhausted from his perilous flight over the top of the dangerous, blue jungle and then on to the capital city, Xethen. Jack, Mutt, Heidi, Vance, and Mr. Amazing had to find another way to get to their critical meeting with the Council of Elders.

As the three kids and Mutt watched, Mr. Amazing snapped his fingers. Five magical and mysterious creatures appeared. The creatures had the body of a horse and their heads resembled that of panda bears. Each of the mysterious creatures was colored like a rainbow and they had white halos over the top of their heads that moved with them as they made their way over to the place where the small group was standing.

"Jack and Mutt, you're going to ride the first two halligans. Their names are Nibbles and Nuggets, and they are half-brothers. They are very gentle, so you will be safe riding them, even though you are novices when it comes to riding."

Mutt barked, and suddenly, leather saddles and bridles appeared on the backs and the heads of the halligans. Mutt levitated up onto the saddle that Nibbles wore and then the magical dog sat down on the saddle. Next, Jack mounted his halligan, Nuggets.

One of the rainbow-colored halligans snorted impatiently and bubbles rose into the air from his nostrils. His halo was brighter than those of the other four halligans.

"This halligan is mine," Mr. Amazing said with authority. The powerful wizard went on to say, "His name is Bubbles for obvious reasons. I will ride directly behind Jack and Mutt."

"What is the name of my beautiful, magical halligan?" Heidi asked Mr. Amazing.

"Your halligan is named Beauty because he is the most handsome. But he can be a handful to ride, so I'm going to have Vance ride right beside you, my dear child. Vance has had riding lessons, so if Beauty starts to act up, Vance will know how to grab Beauty's reins and settle him down," Mr. Amazing said. The magical wizard smiled at Heidi, and he considered her to be the most beautiful of the Earthlings. Therefore, he had matched her up with the most handsome halligan. Knowing Heidi didn't have any experience as to how to mount Beauty, Mr. Amazing snapped his fingers and Heidi rose into the air and was carefully placed on top of Beauty's saddle.

"So, the last halligan is mine," Vance said. "What's his name, Mr. Amazing?"

"Well, your halligan is not the brightest bulb. His name is Clueless!"

Everybody, even the other four halligans, laughed out loud.

"Thanks a lot," Vance managed to say, a look of embarrassment on his freckled face.

"Don't take it personally, Vance," Mr. Amazing said, clearly amused by Vance's reaction. "You see, Clueless needs help with directions from his cousin, Beauty. Clueless lives up to his name because he has no clue as to how to get to the Council of Elders. That's another reason you're going to be riding right beside Heidi. The halligans communicate telepathically. Beauty can give Clueless directions, and then they will walk together because Clueless isn't very brave either."

"That's just great," Vance said with a scowl. He swore under his breath while the others laughed. However, the others were not laughing at Vance, for they weren't mean. Instead, the rest of the group was laughing because of the situation with Clueless. Grudgingly, Vance mounted Clueless. A giant question mark appeared above Clueless's halo because Vance's halligan didn't have a clue as to what was going on. The others had a good belly laugh before the question mark turned into smoke and blew away in the brisk breeze.

"Alright, everyone, it's time to ride over the most dangerous road on Planet Zealon because that's the only way we can get to the magical castle where the Council of Elders is waiting for us. We must ride there quickly because they get impatient easily and we don't want them to get ticked off at us."

About ten minutes later, the group comprised of three Earthlings, five halligans, a powerful wizard, and an extraterrestrial dog arrived at the castle where the Council of Elders was waiting for them. Each Council member came from a different district on Planet Zealon. The members of the Council of Elders were the most powerful wizards from their respective districts. The group of distinguished wizards was all good-looking, highly educated, and brilliant. Their constituents had elected them to the Council of Elders because the group of powerful wizards was the fittest to find solutions to intergalactic challenges. The Council of Elders would reveal important clues so that Jack, Heidi, and Vance could finally solve the mystery they were involved with, and they would also discover what their mission entailed.

Area One was represented by an impressive wizard named Mr. Malloway. He wore a purple robe with gold piping on the sleeves. There was a gold sash tied around his waist. Perched atop his head was a gold, pointed cap covered with images of the Heart Tree.

Area Two was represented by a very tall and slender wizard named Professor McKermott. His robe was blue and green. He wore a cream sash over his right shoulder. He was the youngest of the five Elders, only 9,999 years old! He loved the Heart Tree. He often looked into the magical mirror in his chambers to see the Heart Tree, and to listen to the lullaby the magical, heart-fruit played each evening as the sun started to go down and the puffy clouds turned deep shades of purple, pink, and red.

Area Three was represented by Mr. Humor. He loved children of all ages, but specifically, five to nine-year-old kids. He was best known for his puns and jokes that he loved to share not only with his son, who was five years old, as well as his daughter, who was eight years old, but he also enjoyed joking around with his constituents' kids. Mr. Humor had long, blond hair that was neatly arranged in two braids that hung down the back of his blue and white robe. He wore a soft tam that was made from blue velvet. Mr. Humor was descended from a long lineage of powerful wizards. He wore a proud crest over his right pectoral muscle, which revealed a white emblem depicting a fierce, long-maned, male lion. If a child rubbed the lion's chin, however, the male lion told the youngster a great joke that made them laugh out loud.

Area Four was represented by a changeling named Famous/Brave. When the wizard took his male form, the other Elders in the Council addressed him very respectfully as Famous. When she transformed into a female wizard, she was called deferentially Brave. The Zealonite children loved him/her deeply because Famous/Brave was like having both parents in one wizard-changeling.

Area Five was represented by an exceedingly rare female wizard named Mrs. Happiness. She had no children of her own, choosing instead to surround herself with a menagerie of cats, dogs, bunnies, deer, and huge butterflies that the doting children who followed her all over the place could ride and rest upon during their long walks through the sacred rose gardens that grew around her floating castle in the clouds for as far as the eye could see. Mrs. Happiness was a telepath, and she was closest to Mutt, with whom she often had telepathic communications. The female wizard was dressed in an all sequined, red robe with white piping and wore a large, rose-colored hat with a red and white ribbon that tied neatly beneath her chin.

Mr. Amazing, Mutt, Vance, Heidi, and Jack made their way to the chamber wherein the Council of Elders was awaiting them. The Elders sat in five of the ten available chairs. They were on one side of the table. The table was round and made from dark mahogany wood. The three children, Mutt, and Mr. Amazing sat in the available chairs that were located directly across the table from the Elders.

"Welcome to our meeting, Mr. Amazing and friends," said the five Elders simultaneously.

"We are very happy to be here," Mr. Amazing answered. Mutt and the children nodded their heads in agreement. Mr. Amazing looked at the palm of his right hand to check on Aiden. He saw that his son and Giggles were having a grand old-time swimming together in the gigantic moat that circled the floating castle like a ring.

"So, why are we all gathered here today?" Jack asked, curiosity written on his face.

"Because the Heart Tree is summoning us. You see, you must complete your mission and solve the mystery," Mrs. Happiness explained.

"How do we do that?" Jack asked.

"Look and see!" Famous/Brave said.

Mutt barked once and a beautiful, bejeweled, gold key appeared above the center of the table, then floated over to Jack, who reached up and caught it with his hands. Mutt barked again and an embroidered lanyard appeared directly in front of Jack. Jack picked up the lanyard and attached the key to it and then placed the loop of the lanyard around his neck.

"What do I use this key for?" Jack asked.

"It's a clue to solving the mystery. You'll find out later on," Professor McKermott said.

"How do we get to the Heart Tree?" Jack asked.

"We are going to take there chairs," Mr. Humor said. "You sit in the there chair and it takes you to whatever destination you want to go to. In this case, our there chairs will take us directly to the Heart Tree. Homeostasis is maintained. Space suits are not needed because a there chair has a built-in atmosphere surrounding it," Mr. Humor explained.

Mutt barked loudly. Ten there chairs appeared in a line. The five Council members, Mr. Amazing, Jack, Heidi, Vance, and Mutt took their seats in their respective there chairs. Mutt barked again and they appeared in front of the Heart Tree.

A stone wall and an iron gate surrounded the Heart Tree.

"Jack, I want you to take the key and open the gate with it. You are the only one who can open the gate. This is why you have been brought to Planet Zealon! We are going to help your Planet Earth," Mr. Malloway said.

The heroic Jack did exactly what he was told. He got up out of his there chair and made his way over to the front of the gate. He removed the lanyard from around his neck, inserted the key into the lock of the gate, and finally turned the key to the right.

The stone wall and the front gate disappeared.

All of them gathered around the Heart Tree, holding hands, and feelings of joy and wonder flooded through the connected circle of friends. Next, something marvelous happened as they joined voices. They sounded like the most beautiful choir imaginable; harmonious and otherworldly. Their song started low, and then quickly gained momentum. The song they sang filled the air with happiness.

Meanwhile, the Heart Tree transformed into the most gorgeous, sun-like being. Golden rays shot out from the ends of his branches. The entire sky was filled with beautiful, warm light. Then, each being that held hands in the magical circle surrounding the Heart Tree began emitting red, orange, yellow, green, blue, indigo, and violet colors from their faces. A beautiful rainbow circled high above the Heart Tree.

The song became louder. As it did so, the golden light from the Heart Tree intensified, as did the rainbow that was located high above the magical, sacred tree.

This was the joyful song they sang together:

> Happy is this day we find,
> When climate change is now behind.

The future fills us all with glee,
We've saved the Earth, forever be.
The sister Planet that we find,
A gorgeous chance for love and mind.

The Council Elders, Mutt and Jack, along with Heidi and Vance, and of course, Mr. Amazing and his soon-to-be-crowned king/son Aiden, sent a telepathic message to Earth that summarized what everyone circled around the Heart Tree was thinking and feeling.

Save Earth.

Save us.

Printed in the United States
by Baker & Taylor Publisher Services